THE BRAIN STORM

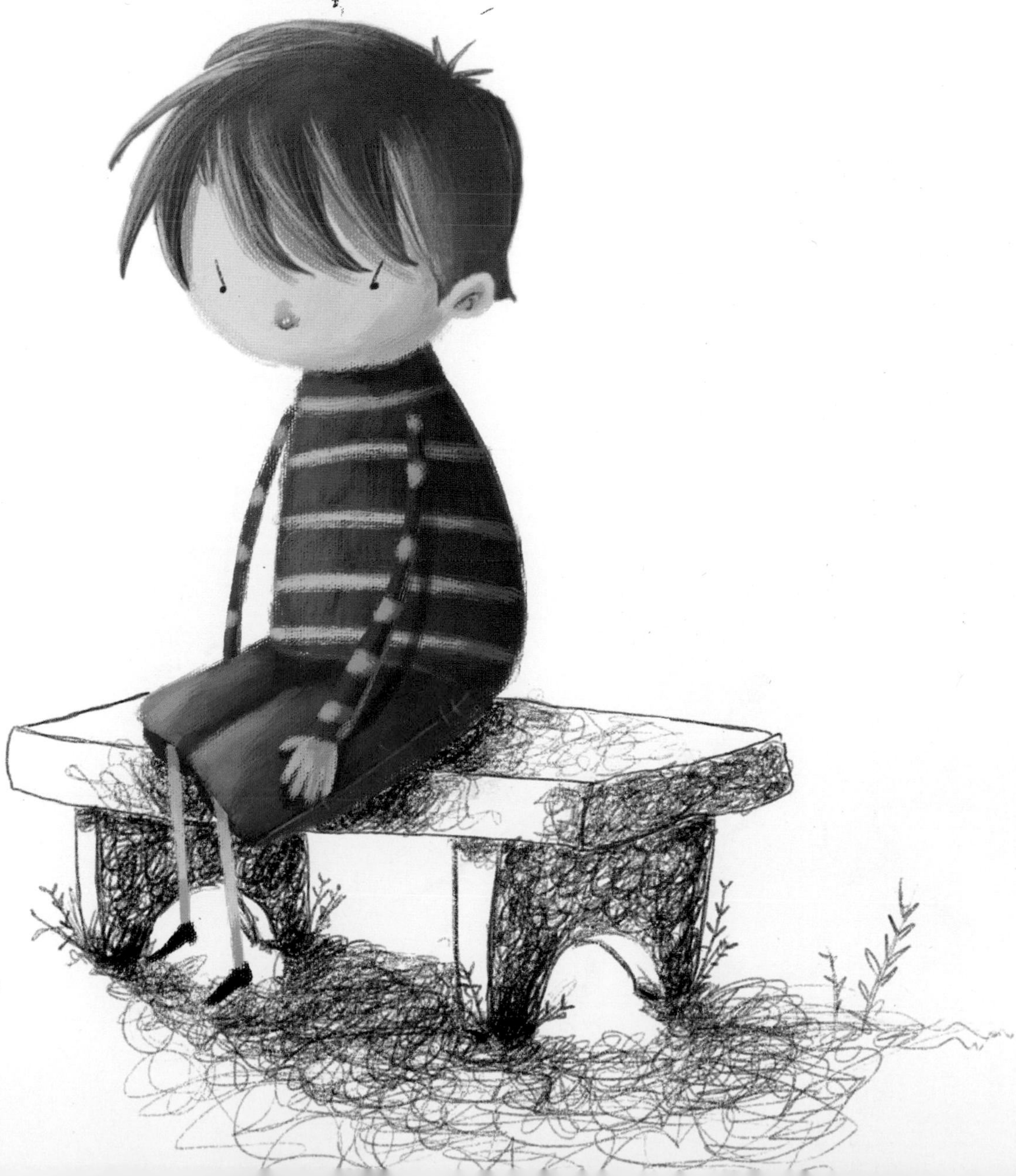

Unwritten by Linda Ragsdale
Illustrated by Claudio Molina

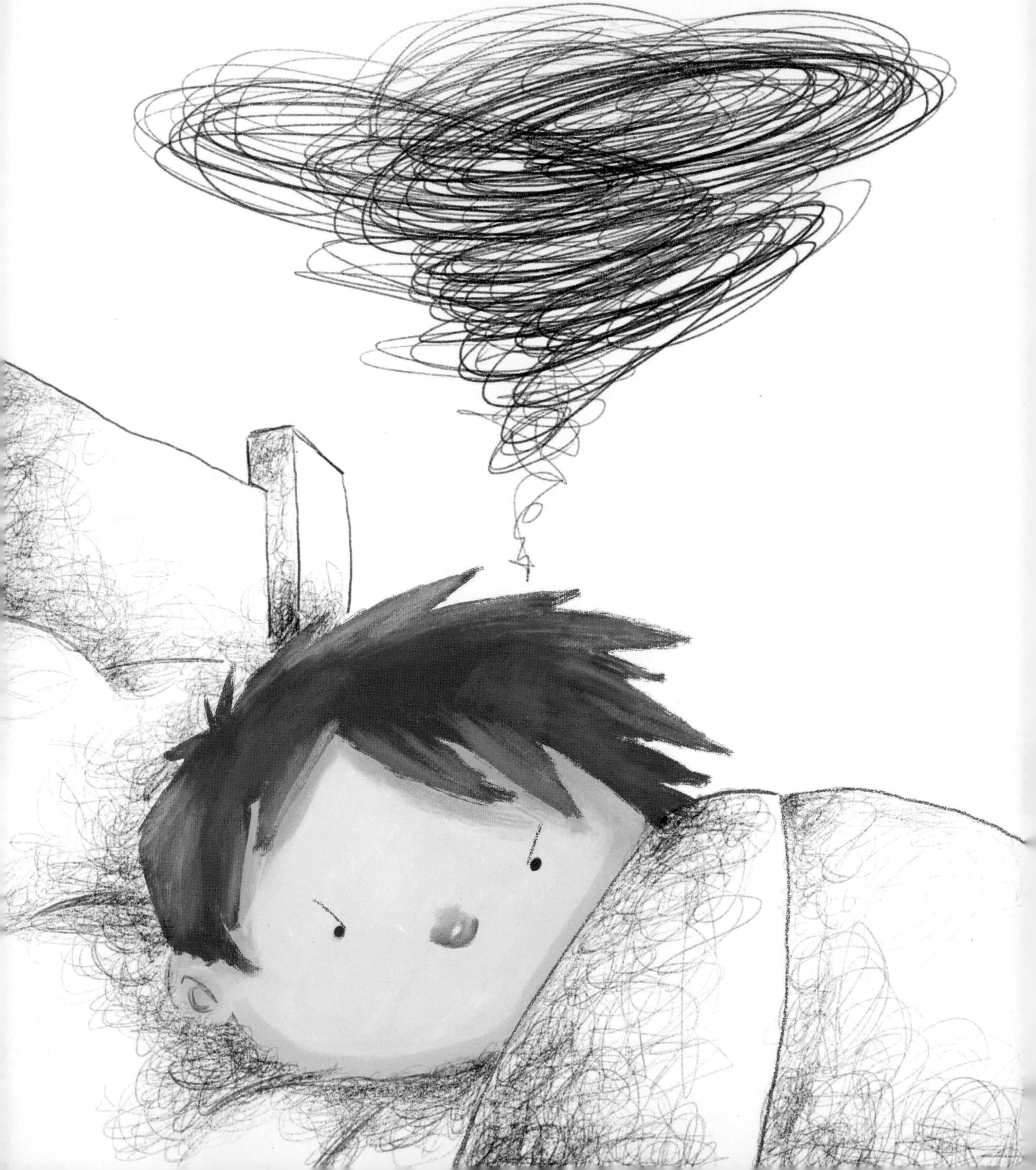

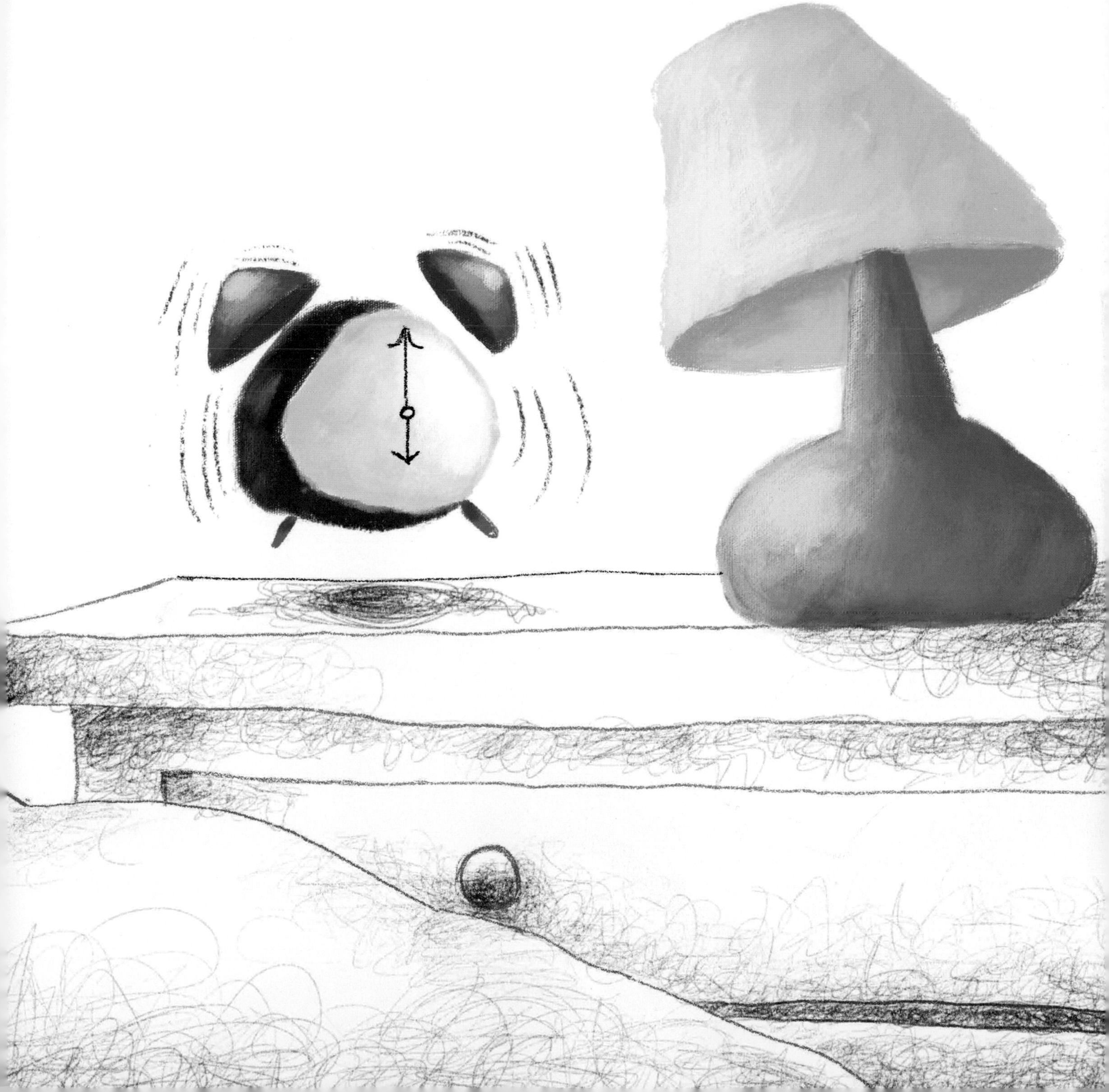

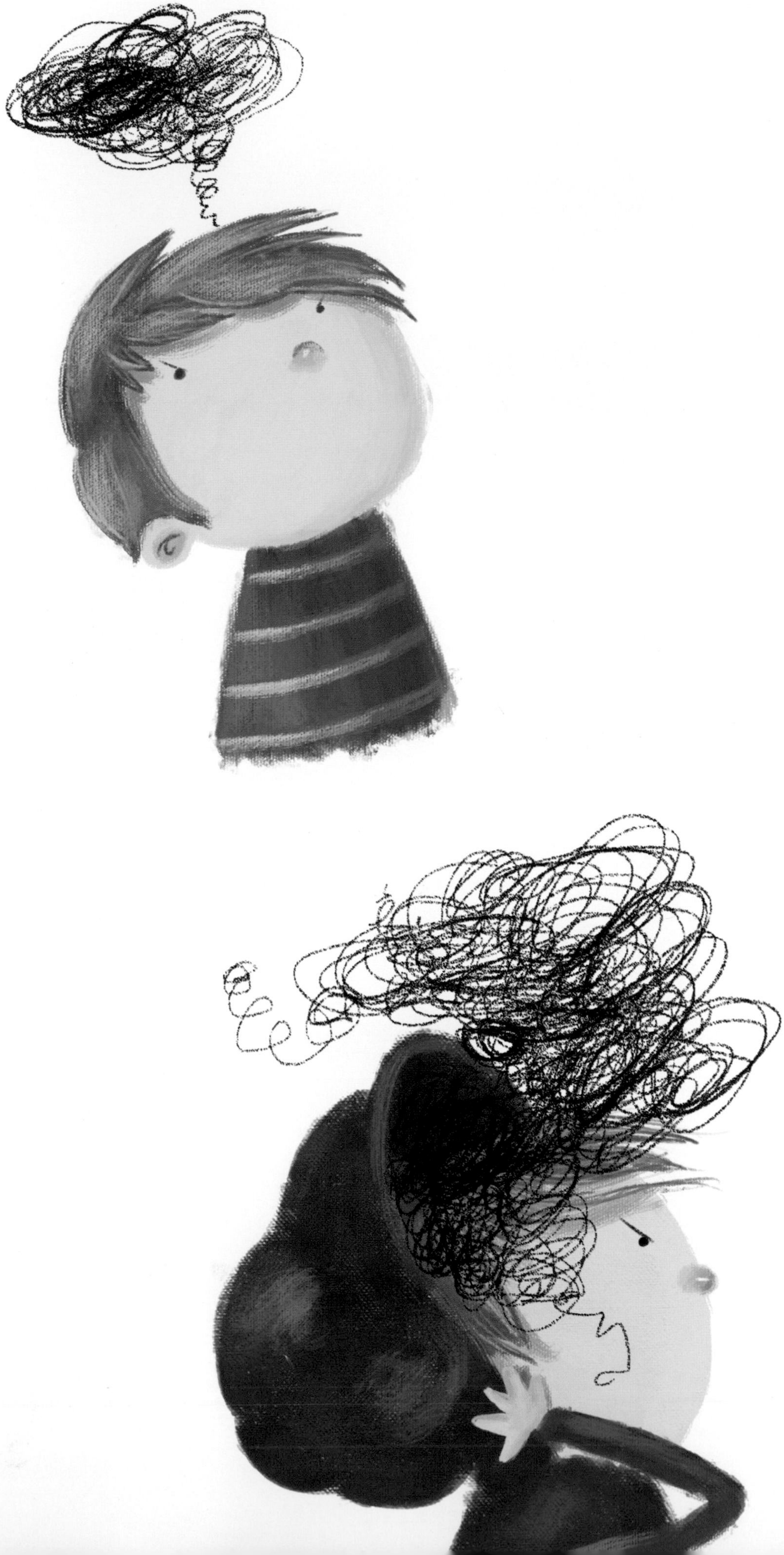

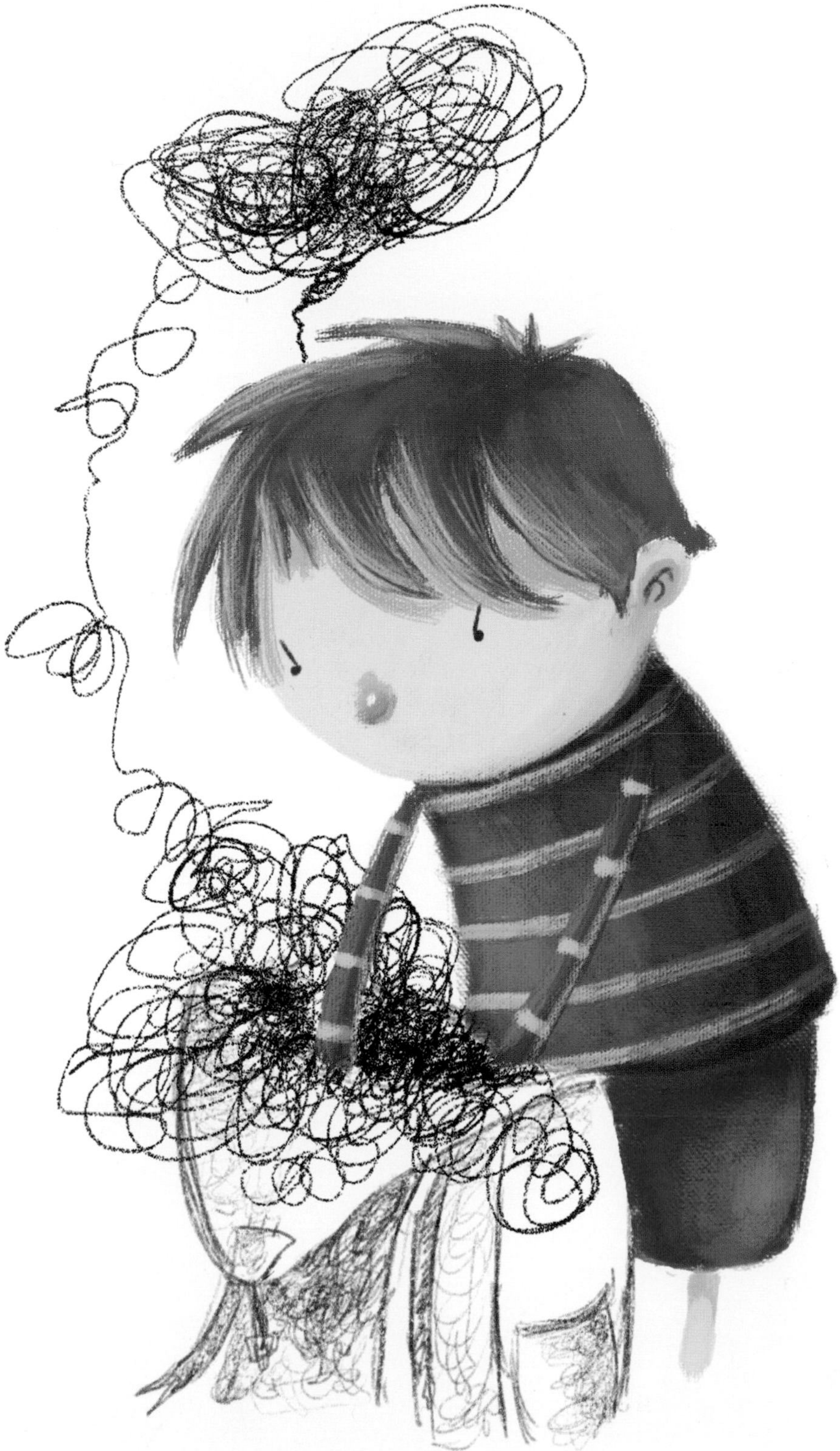

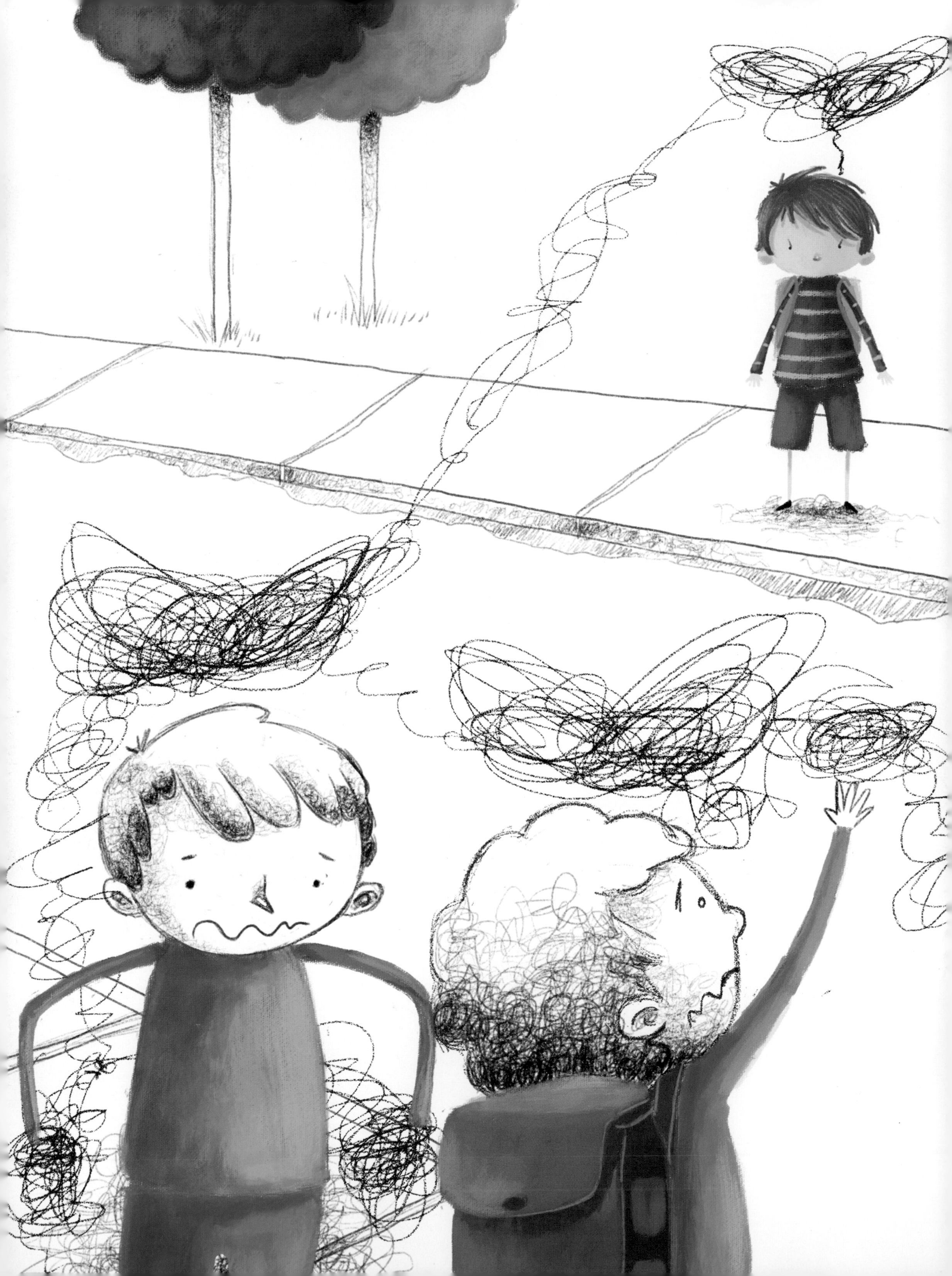

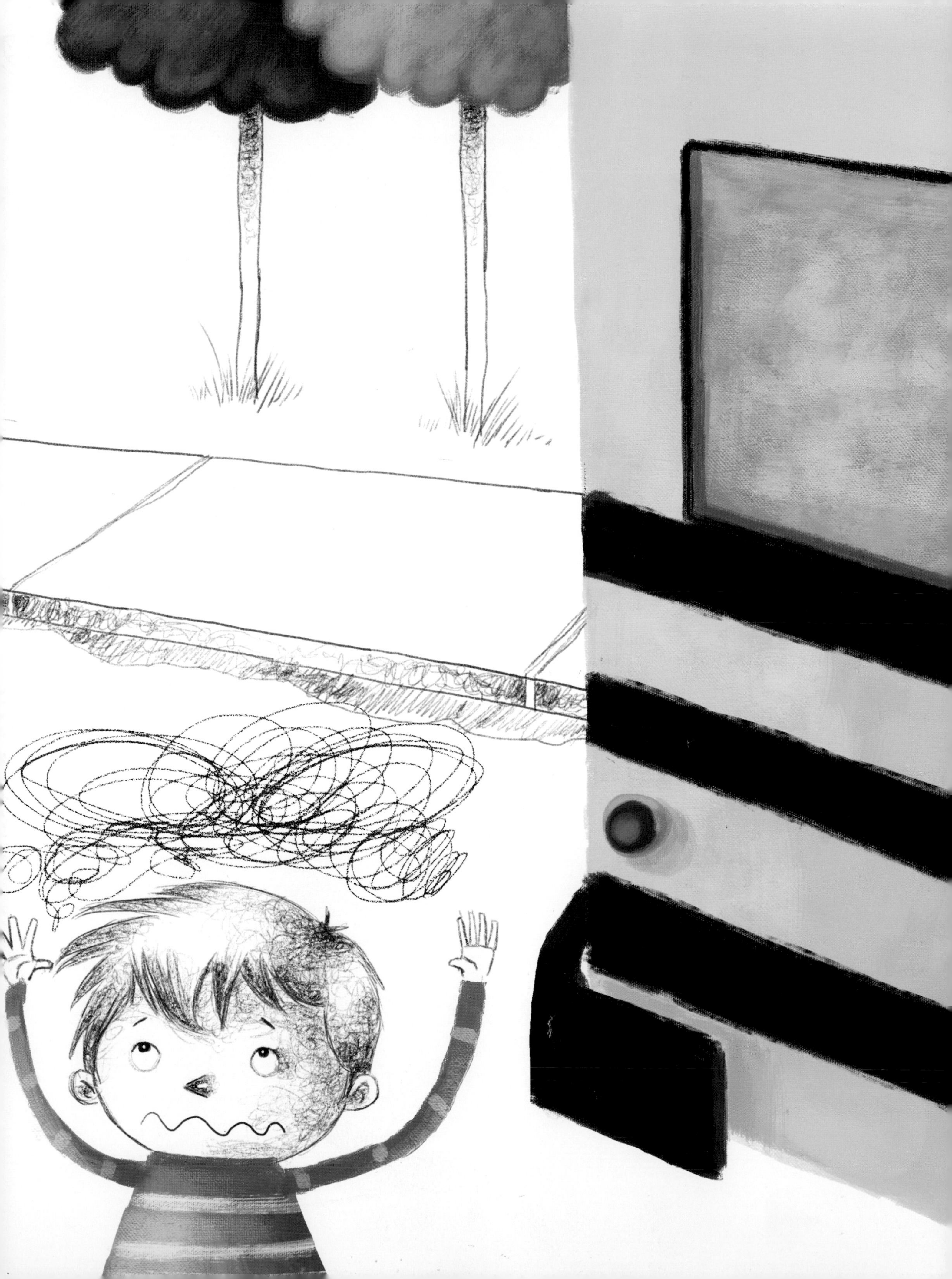

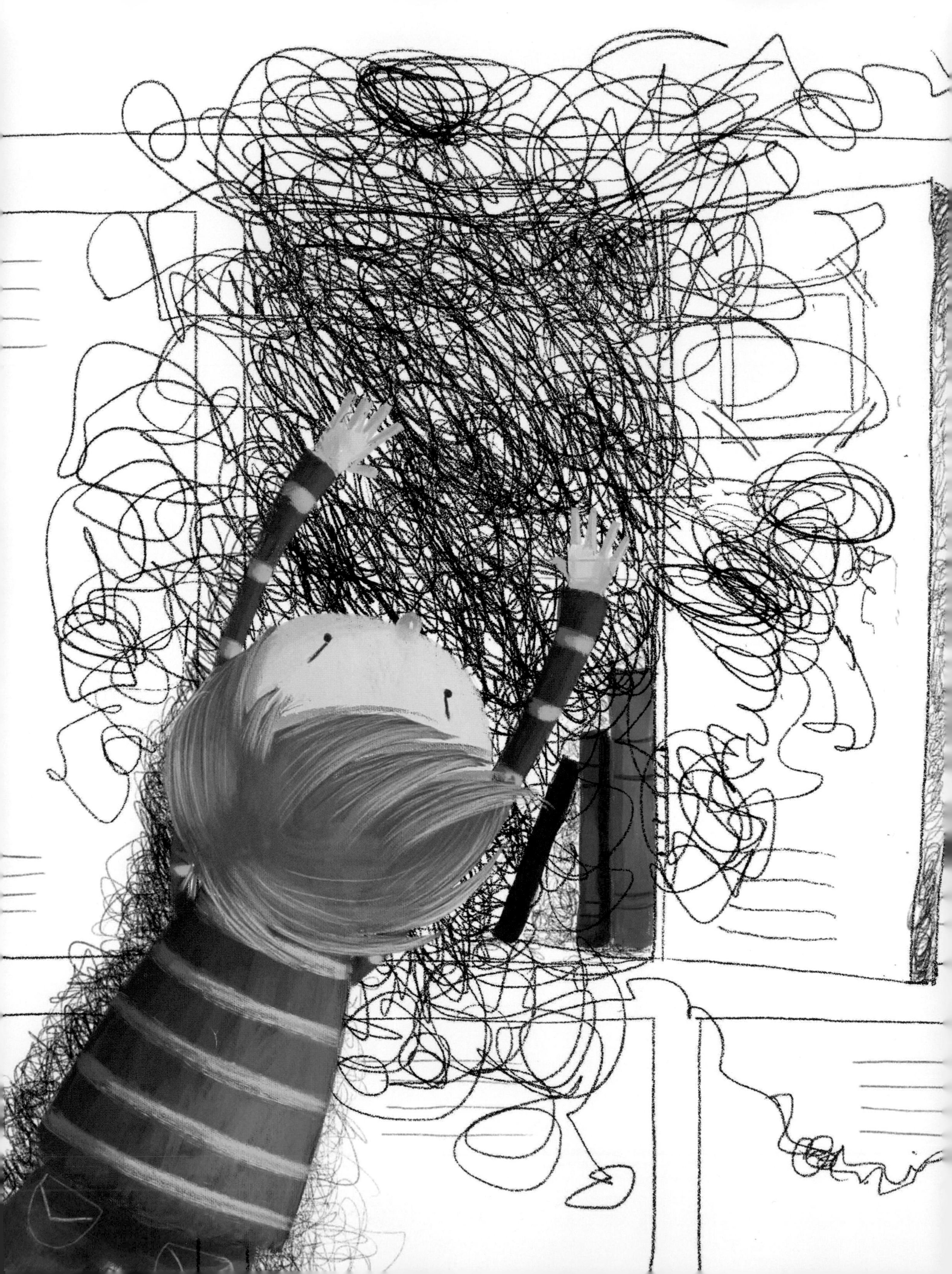

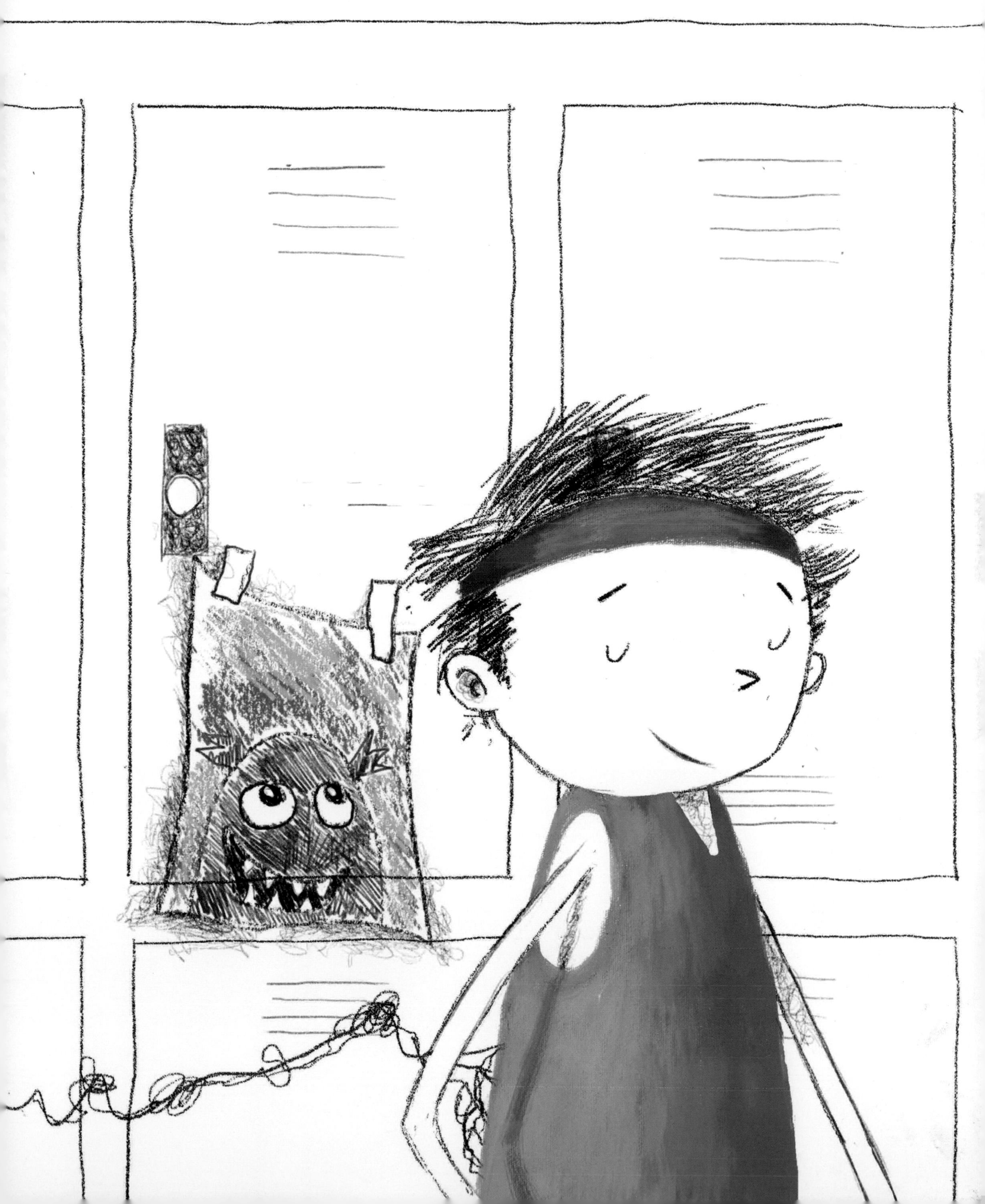

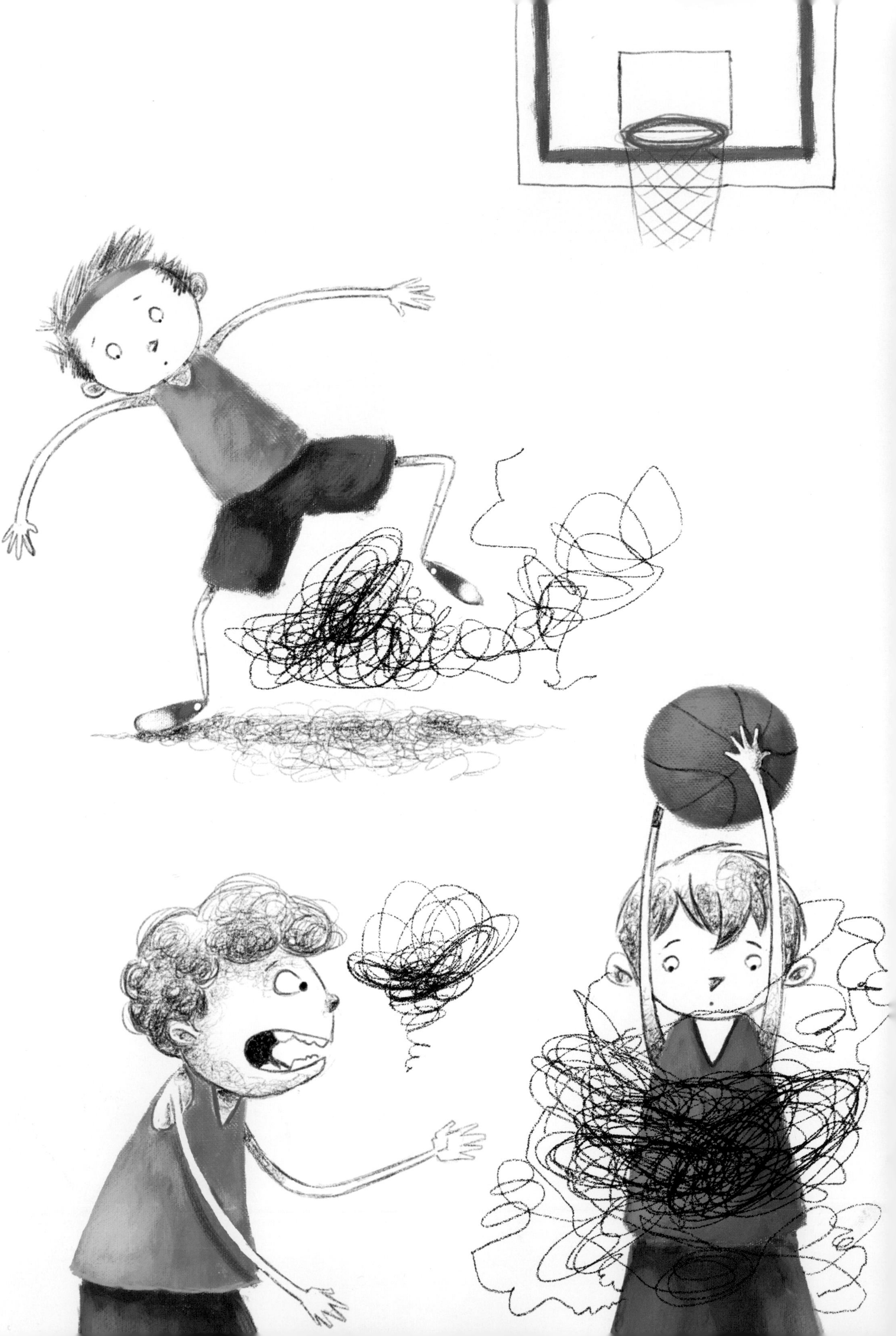

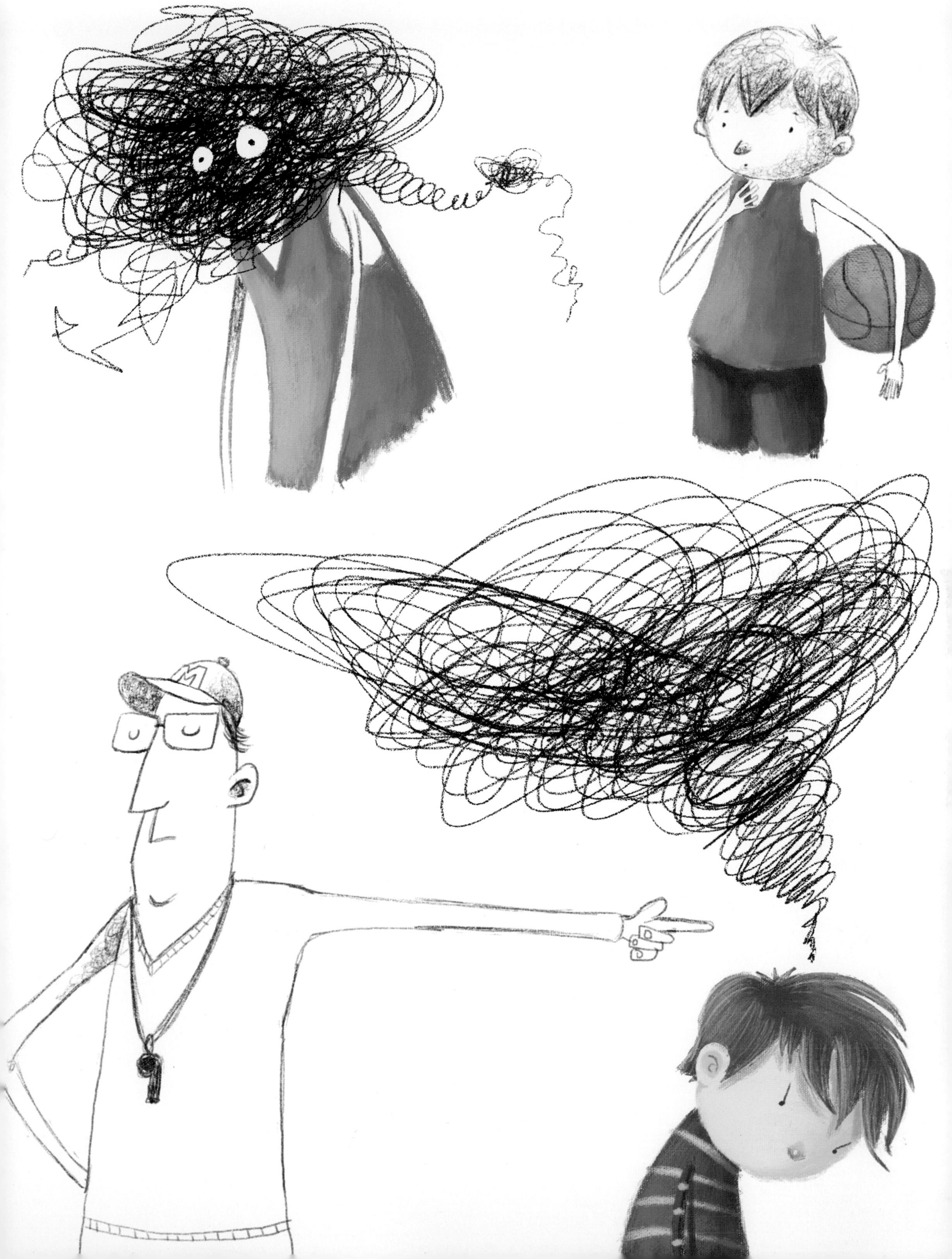

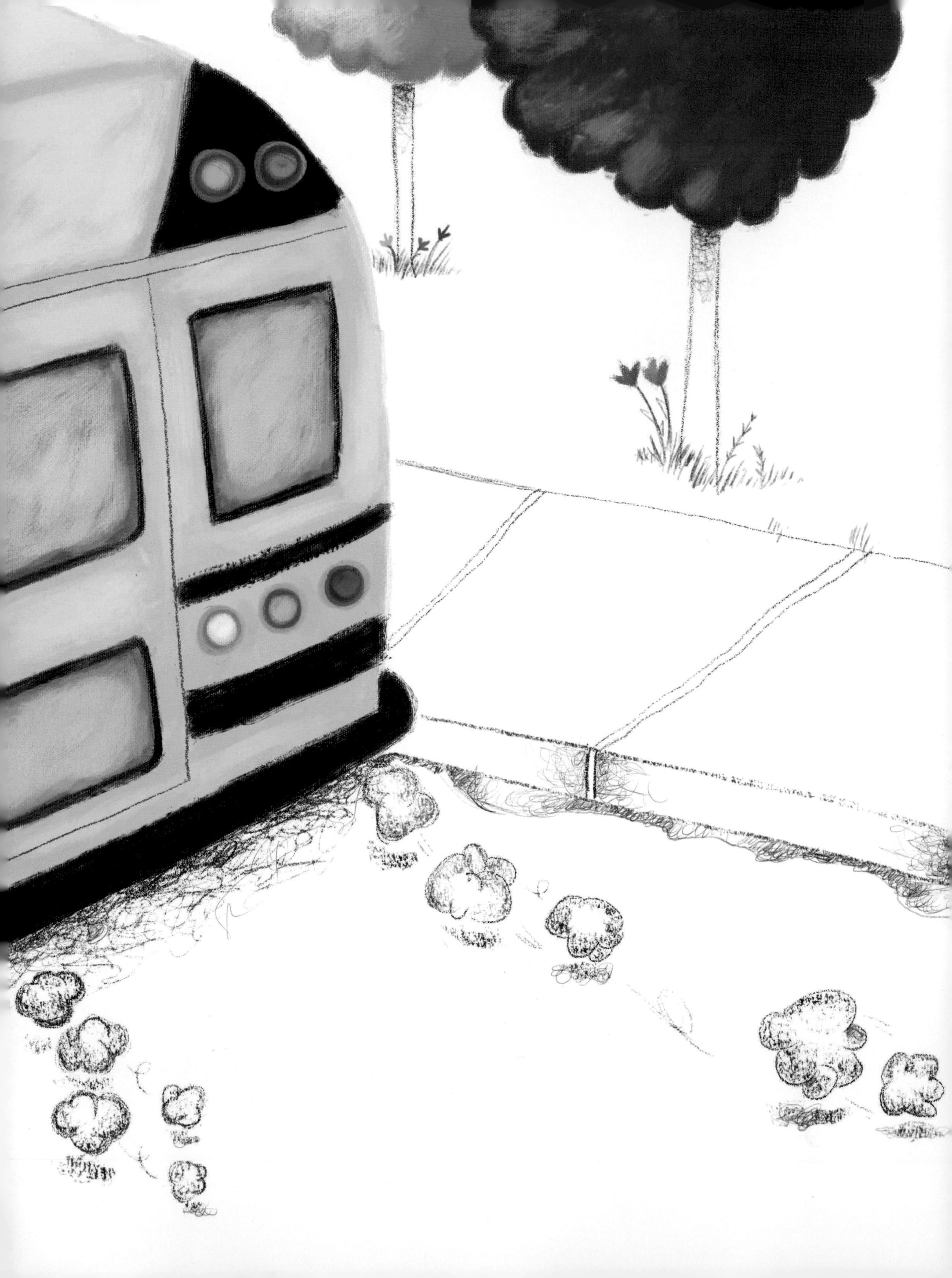

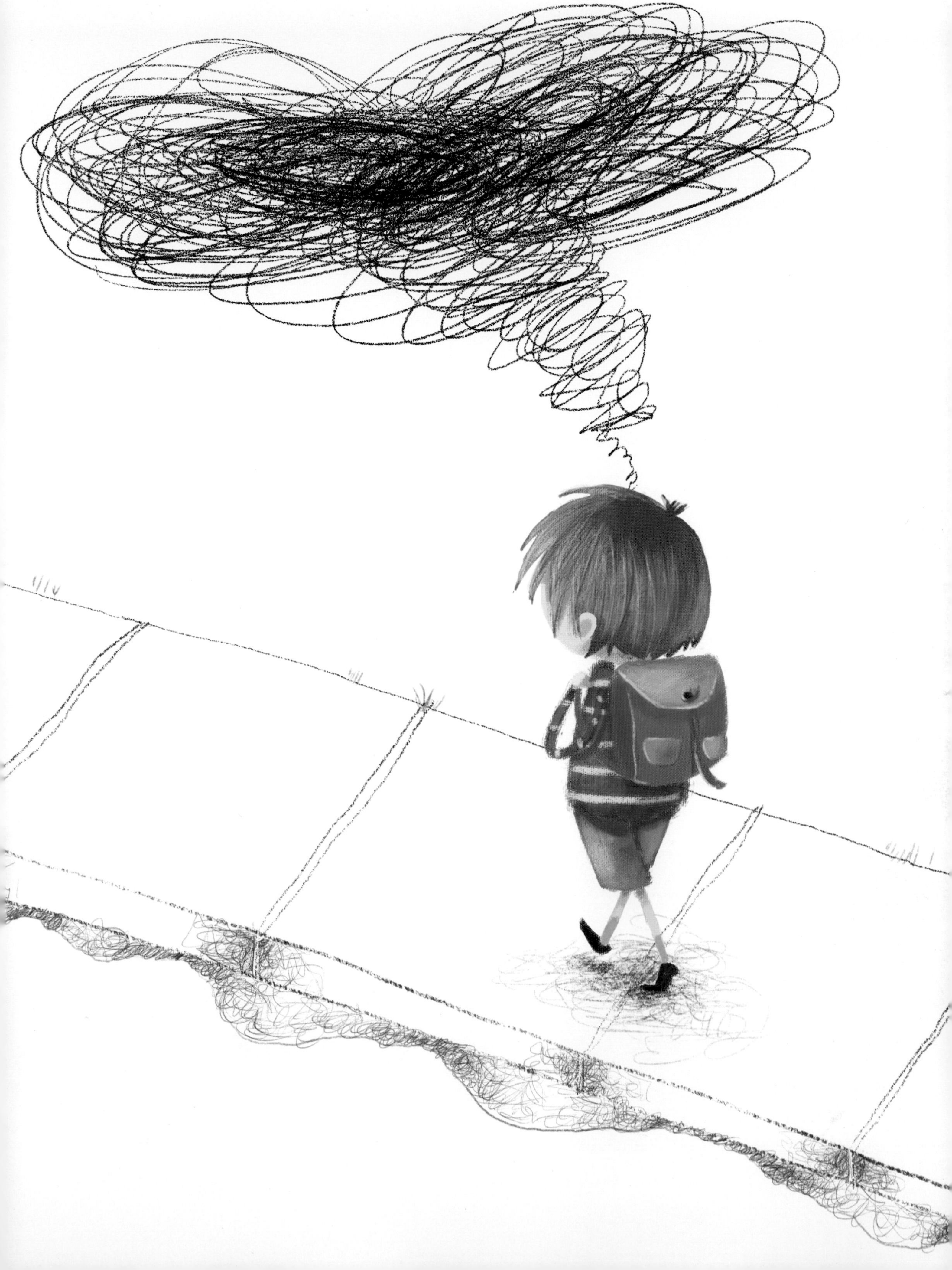

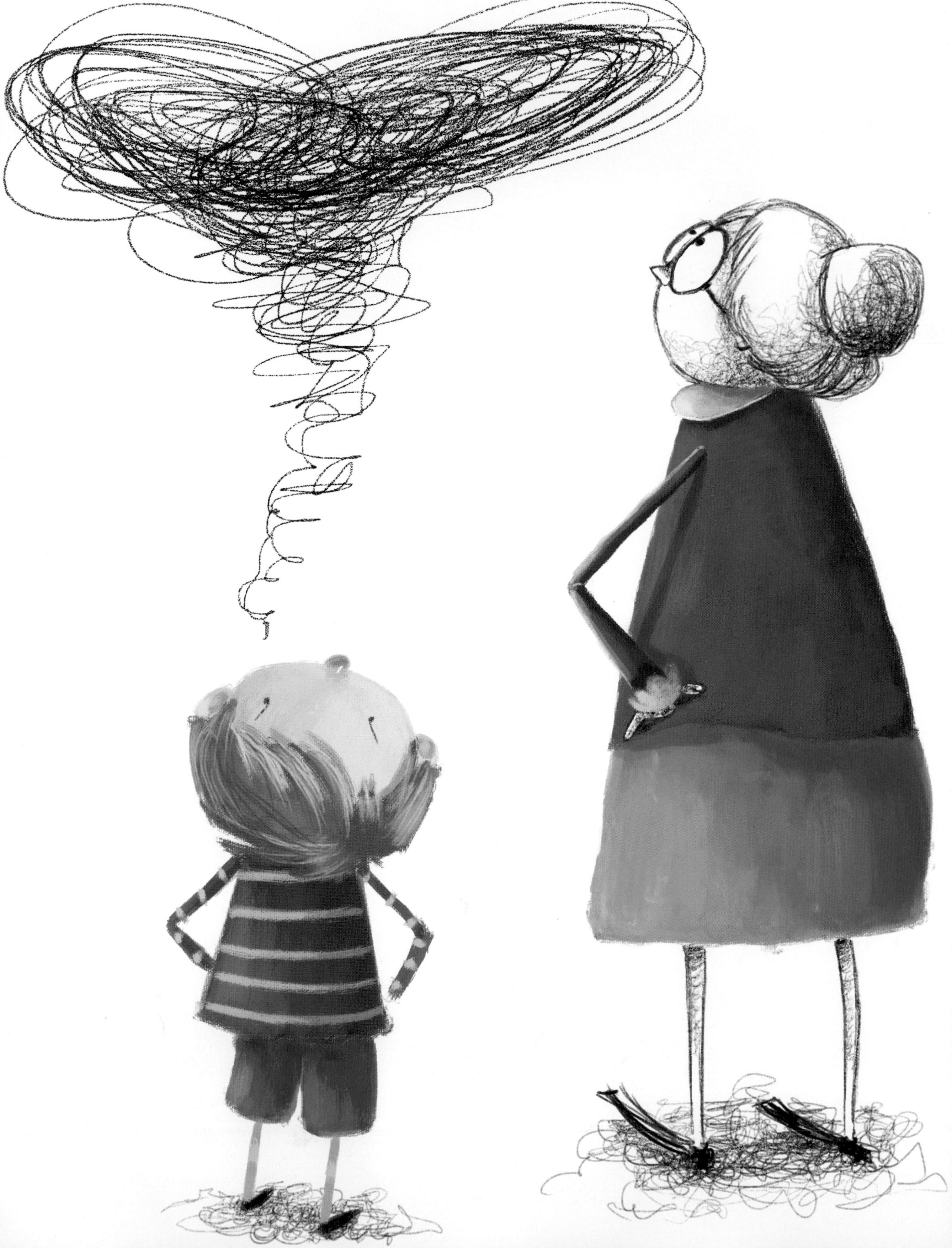

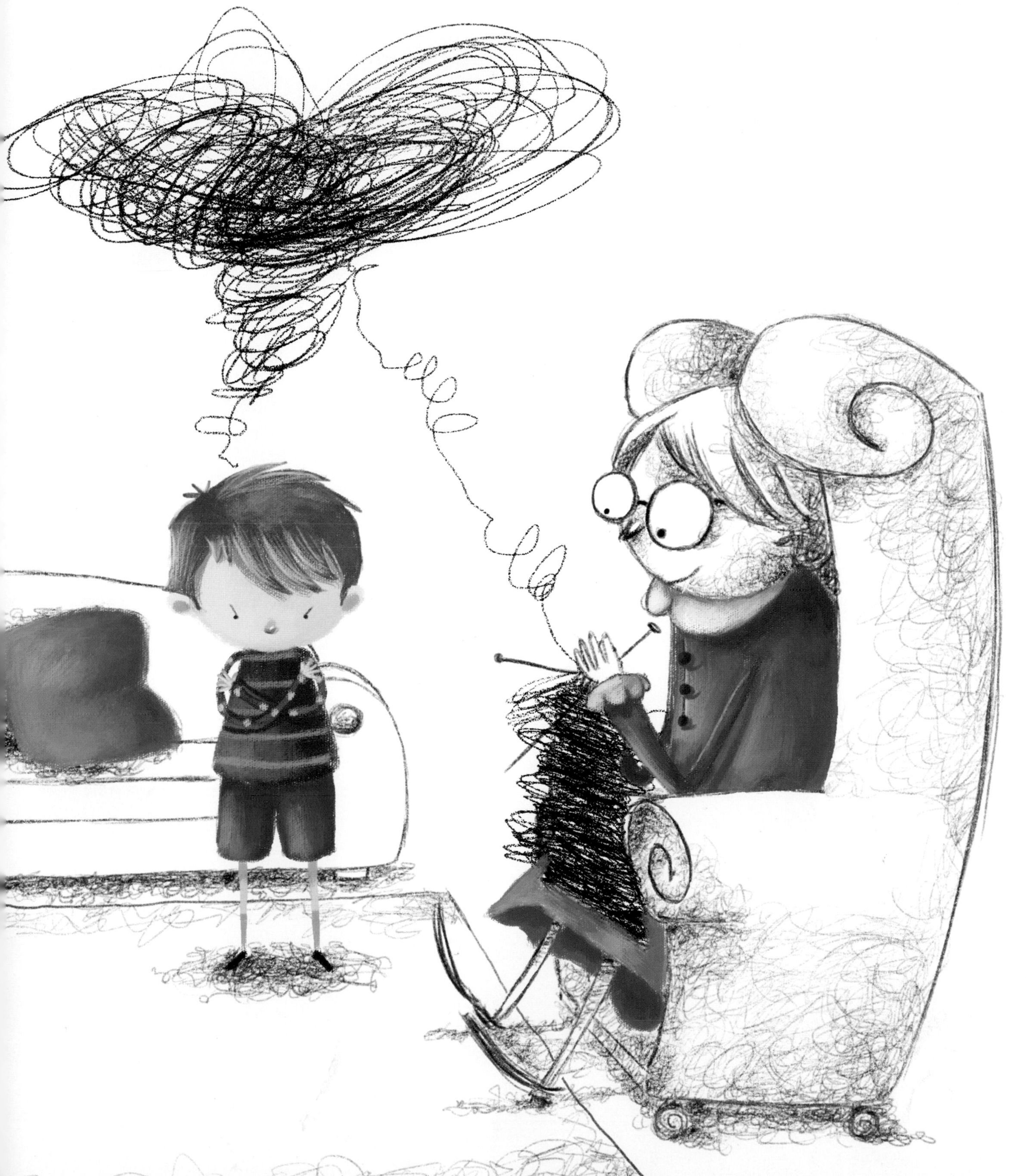

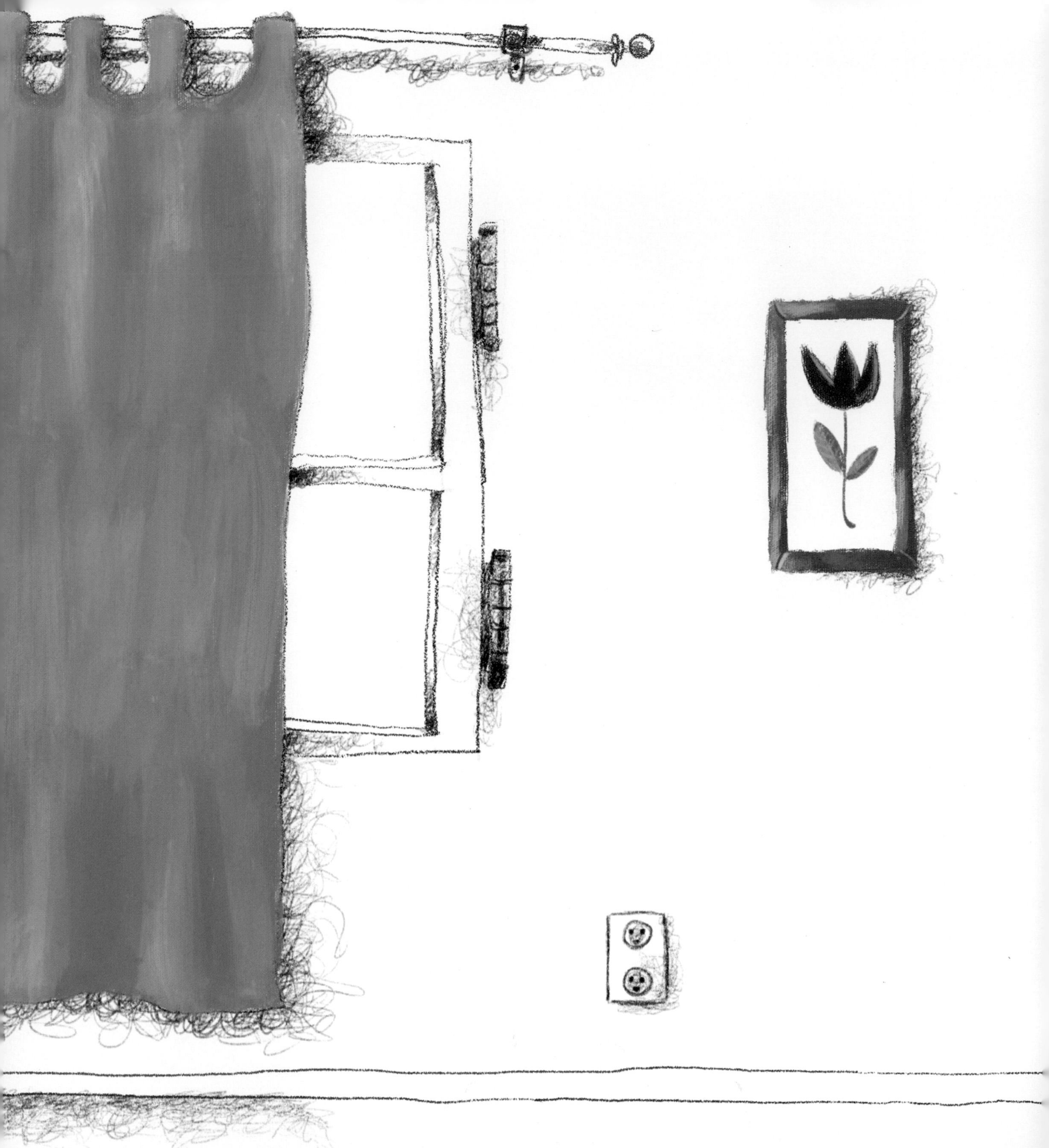

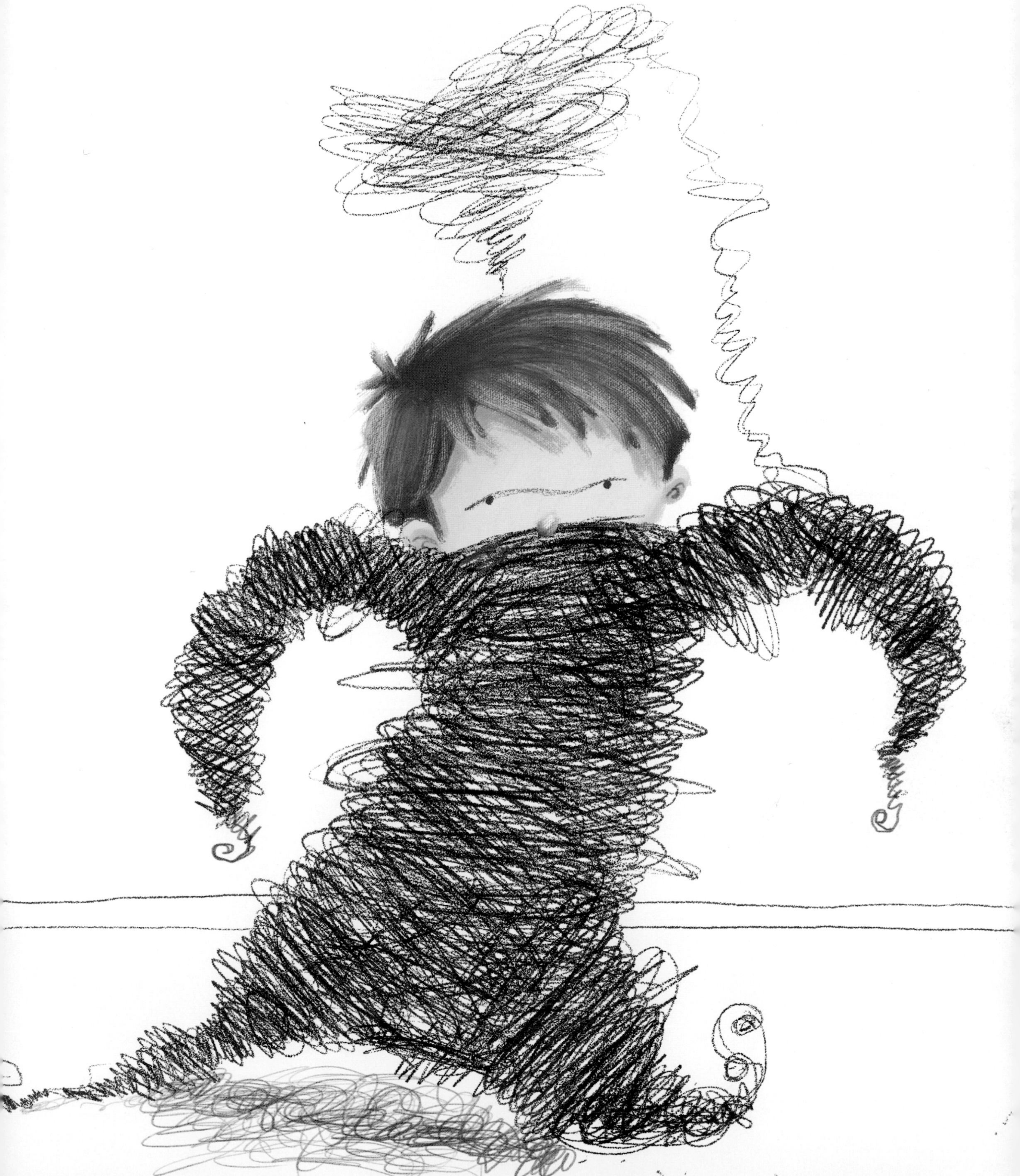

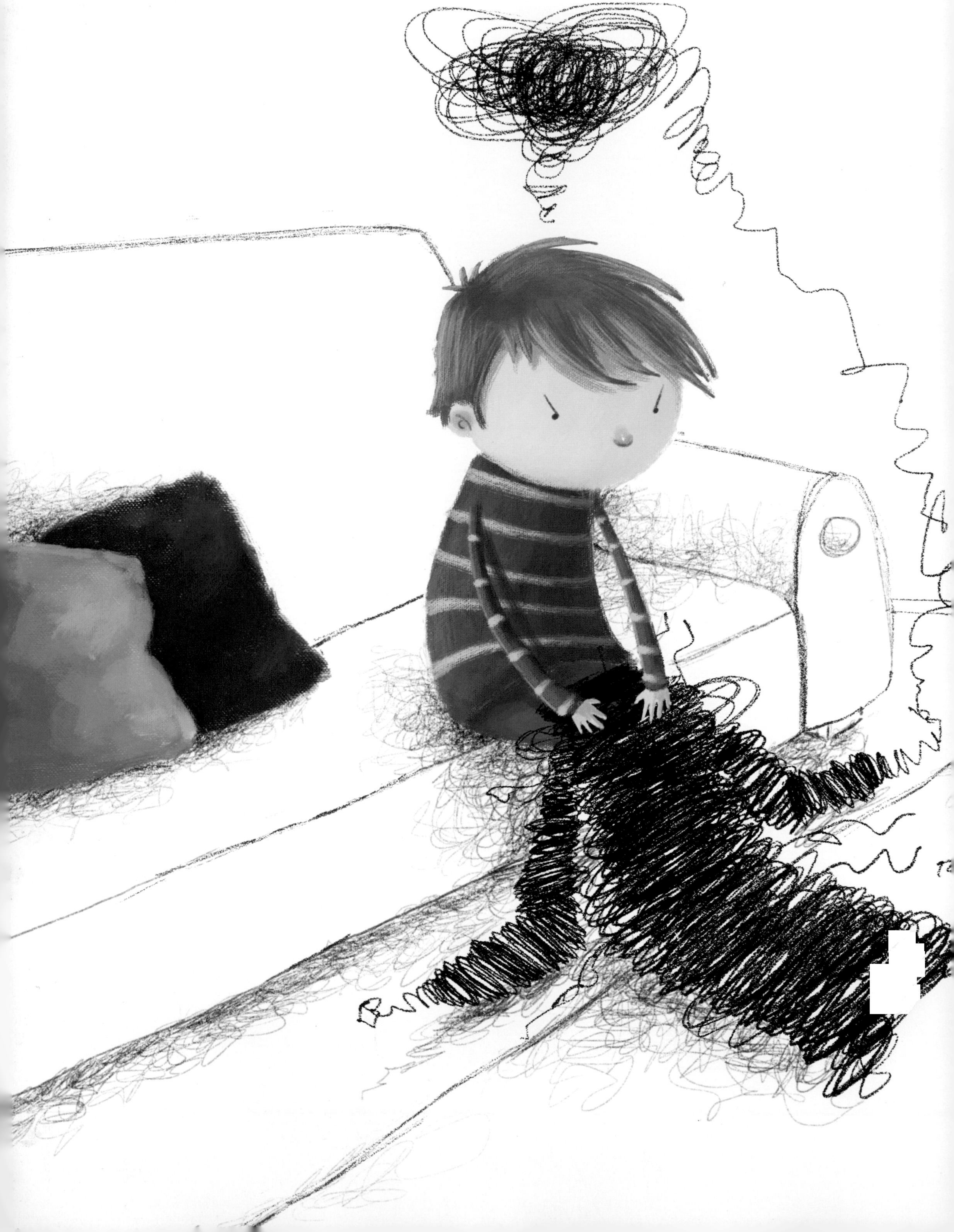

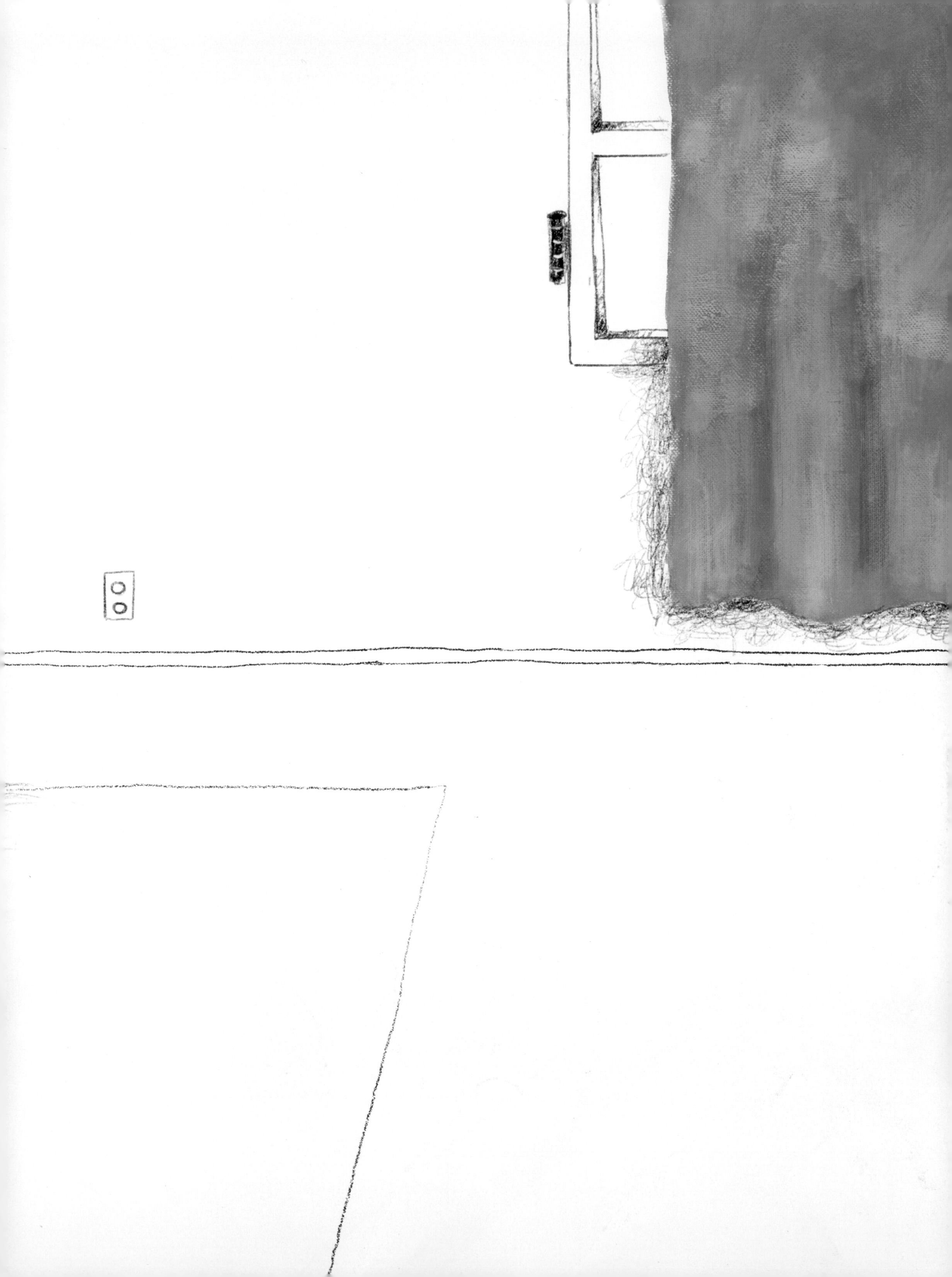

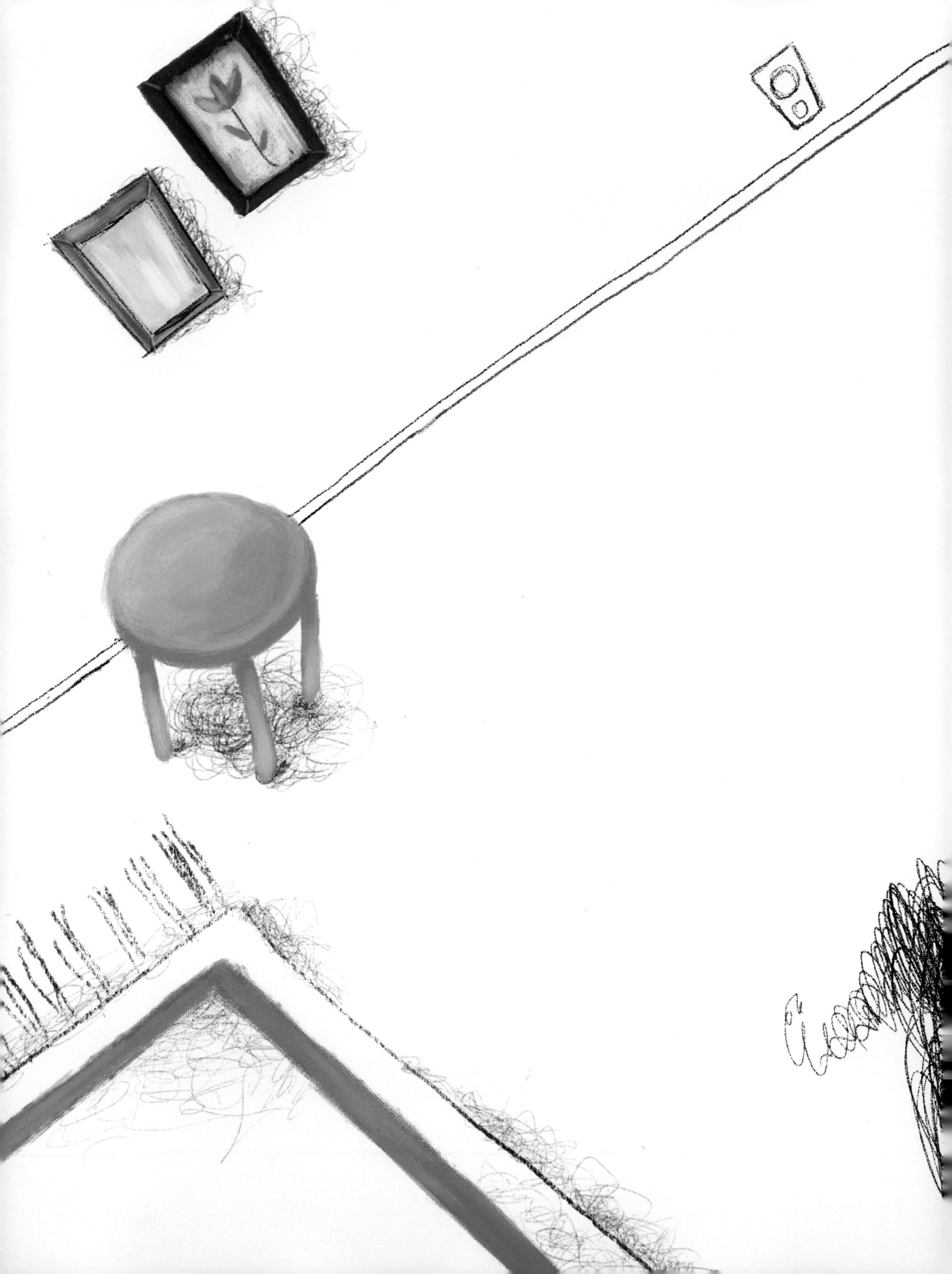

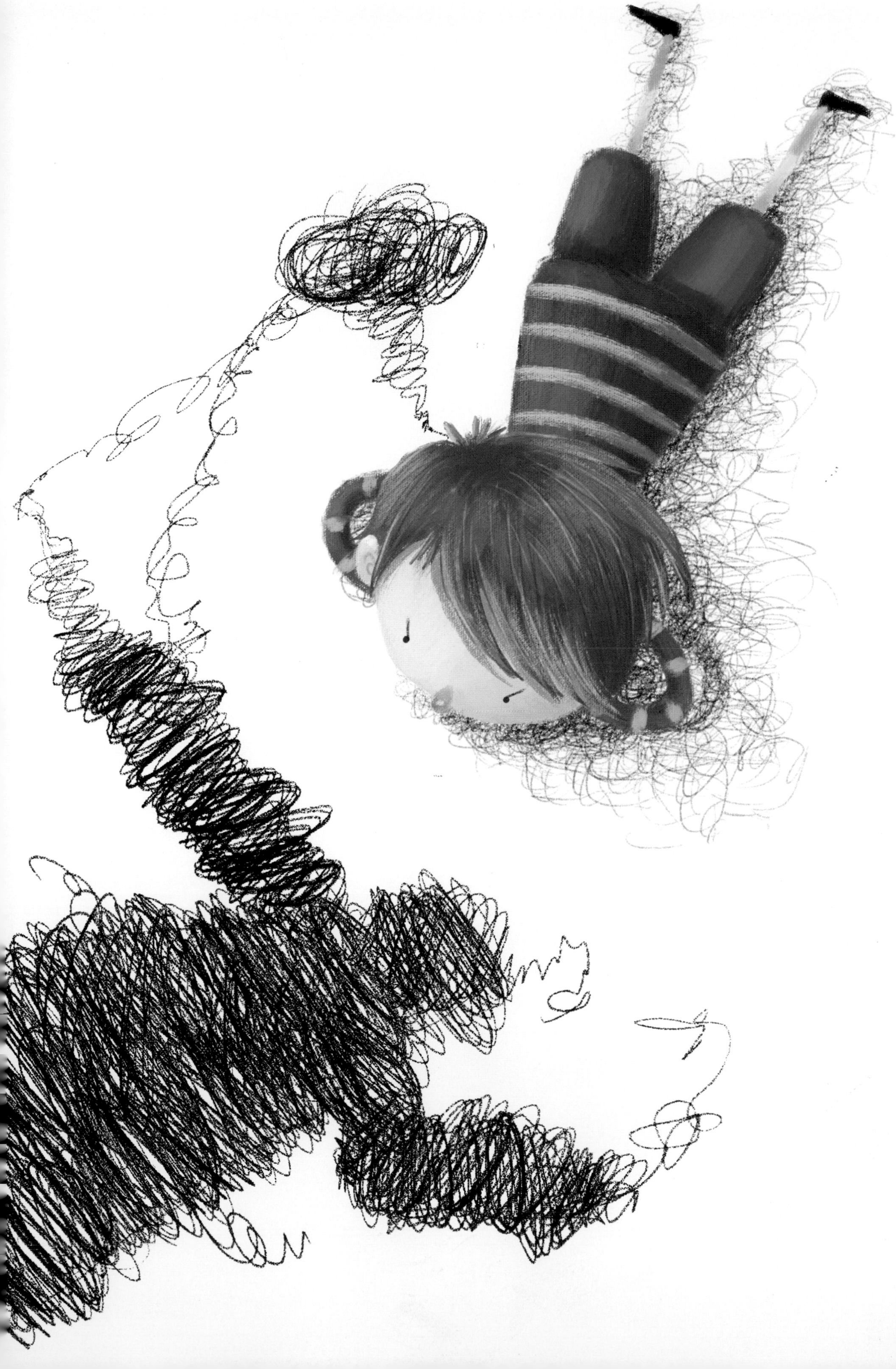

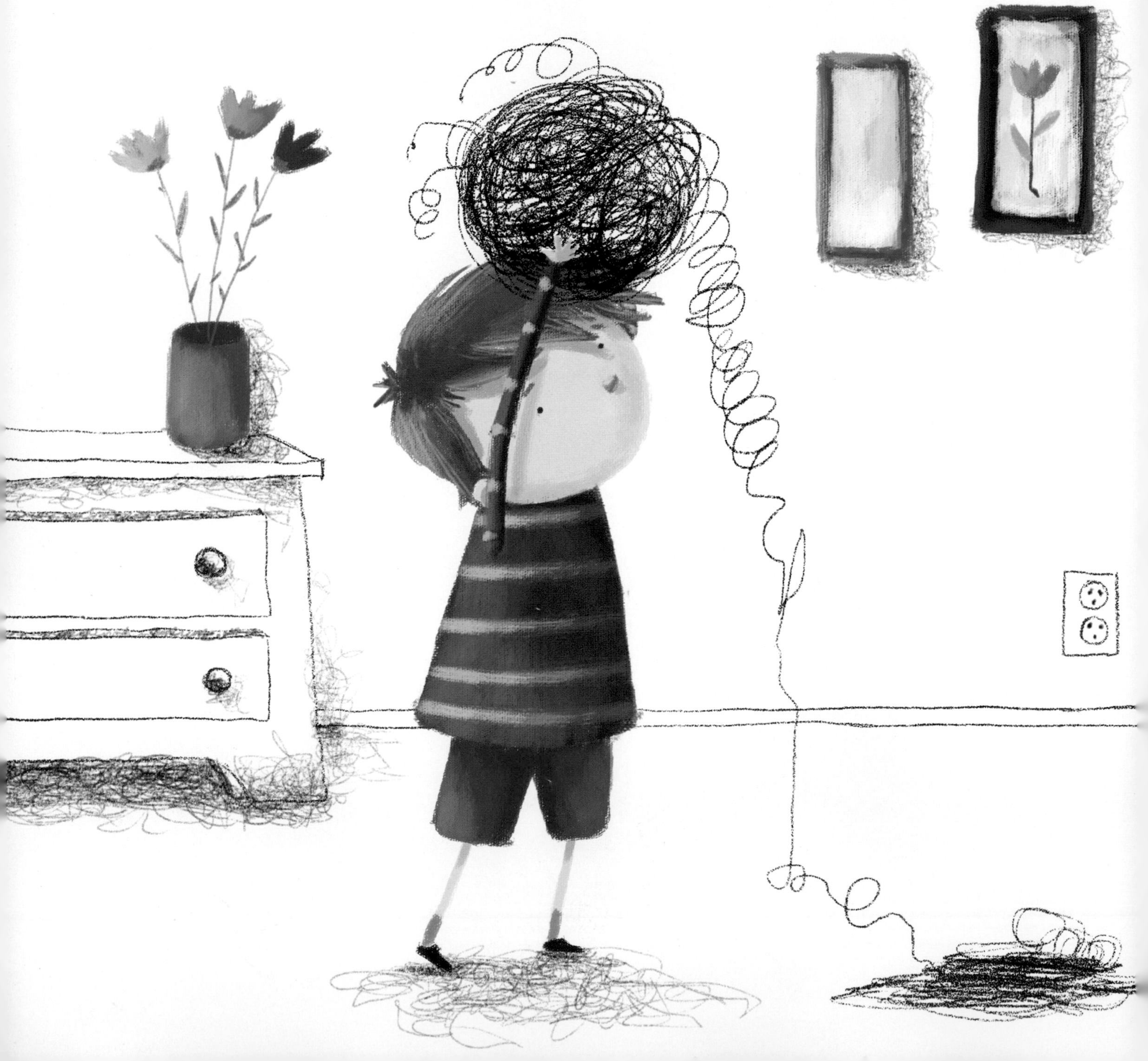

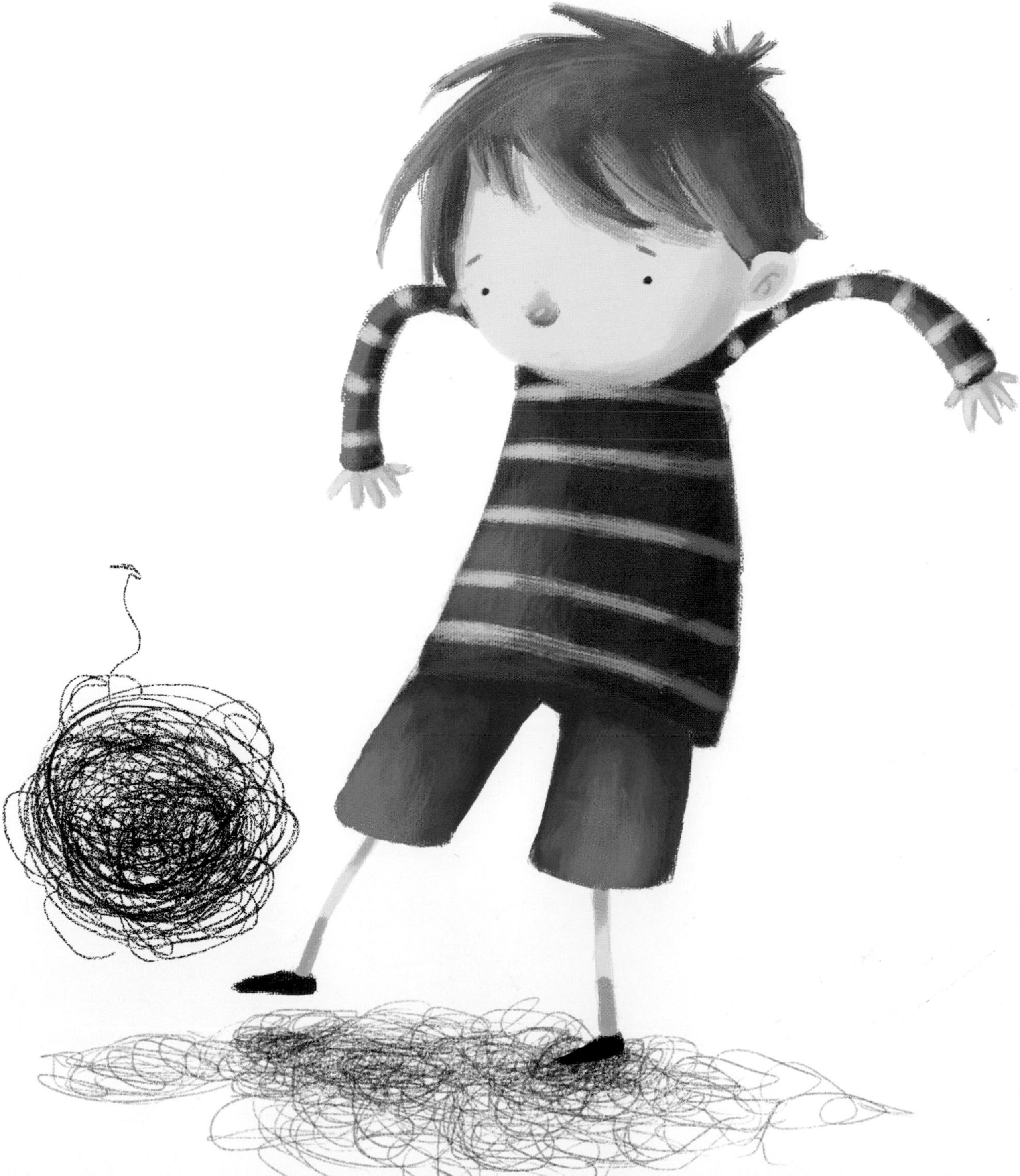

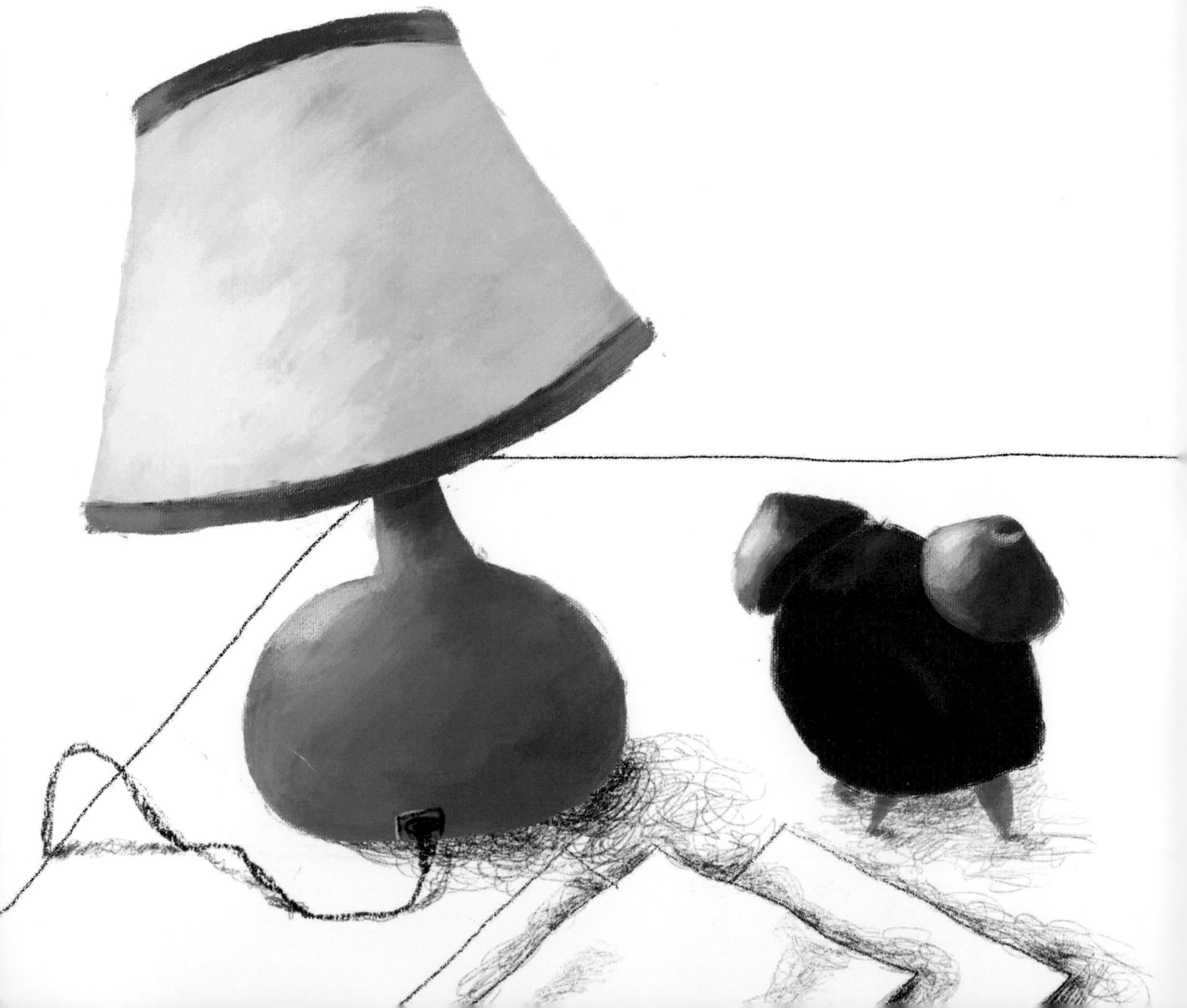

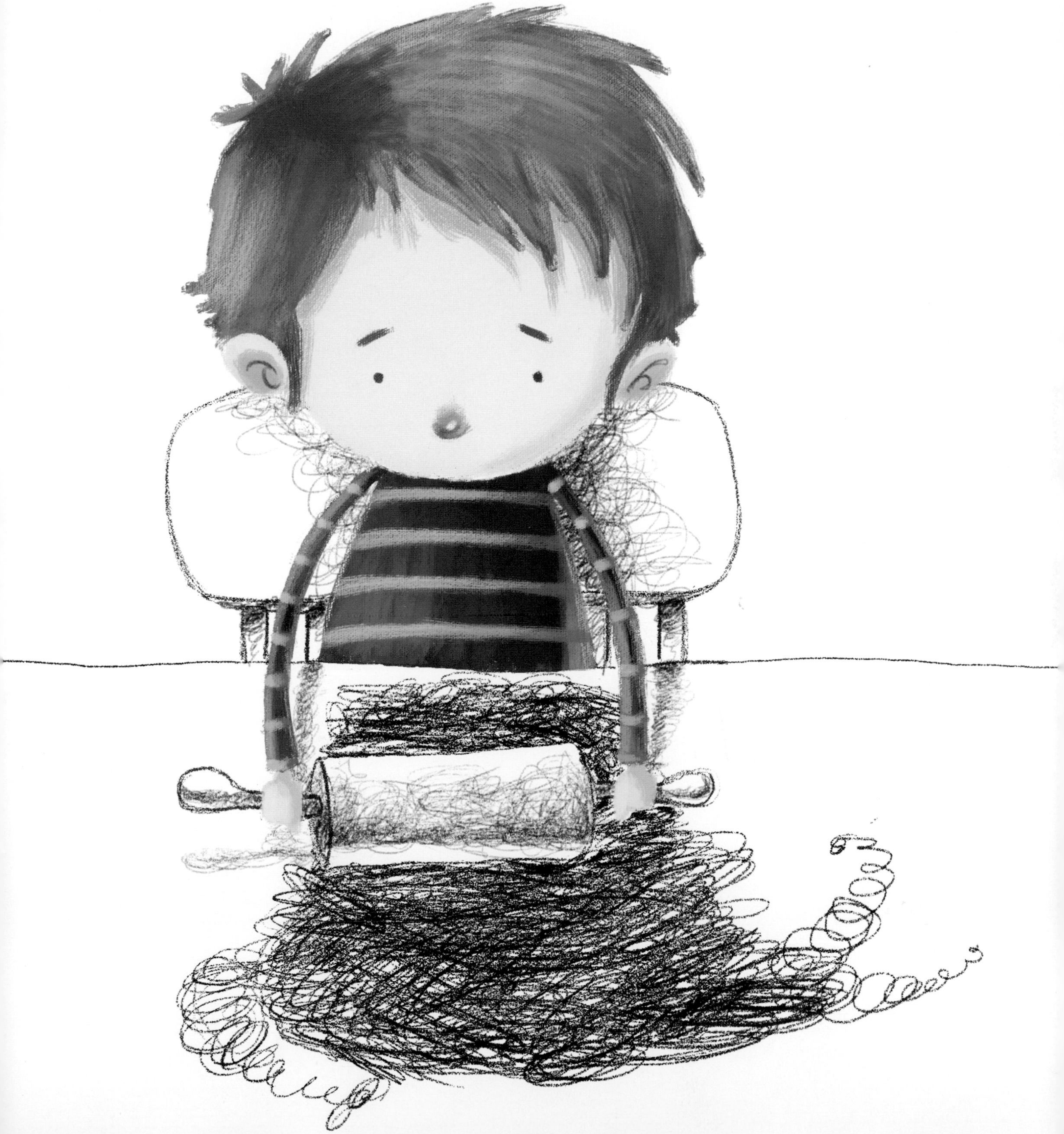

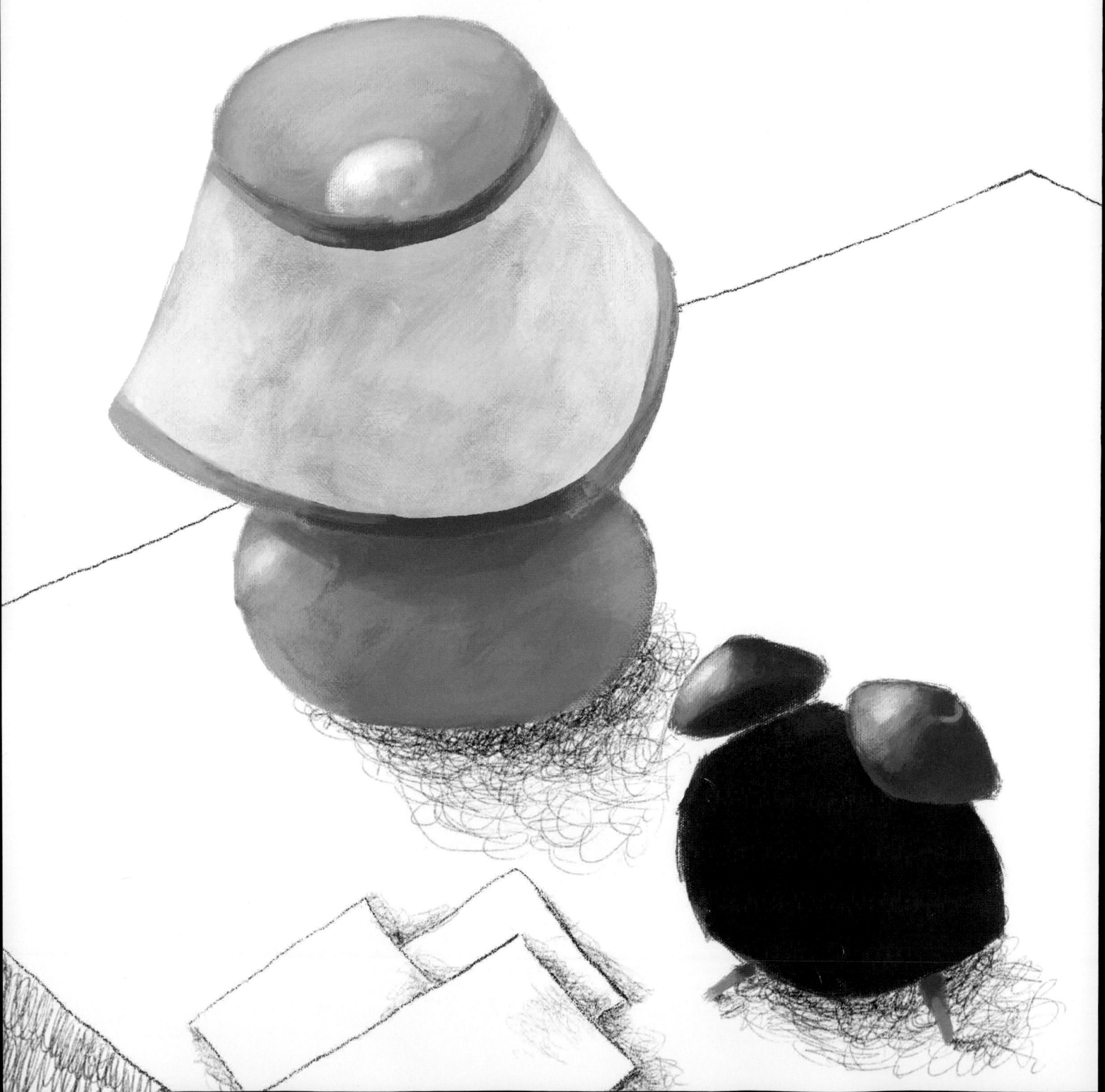

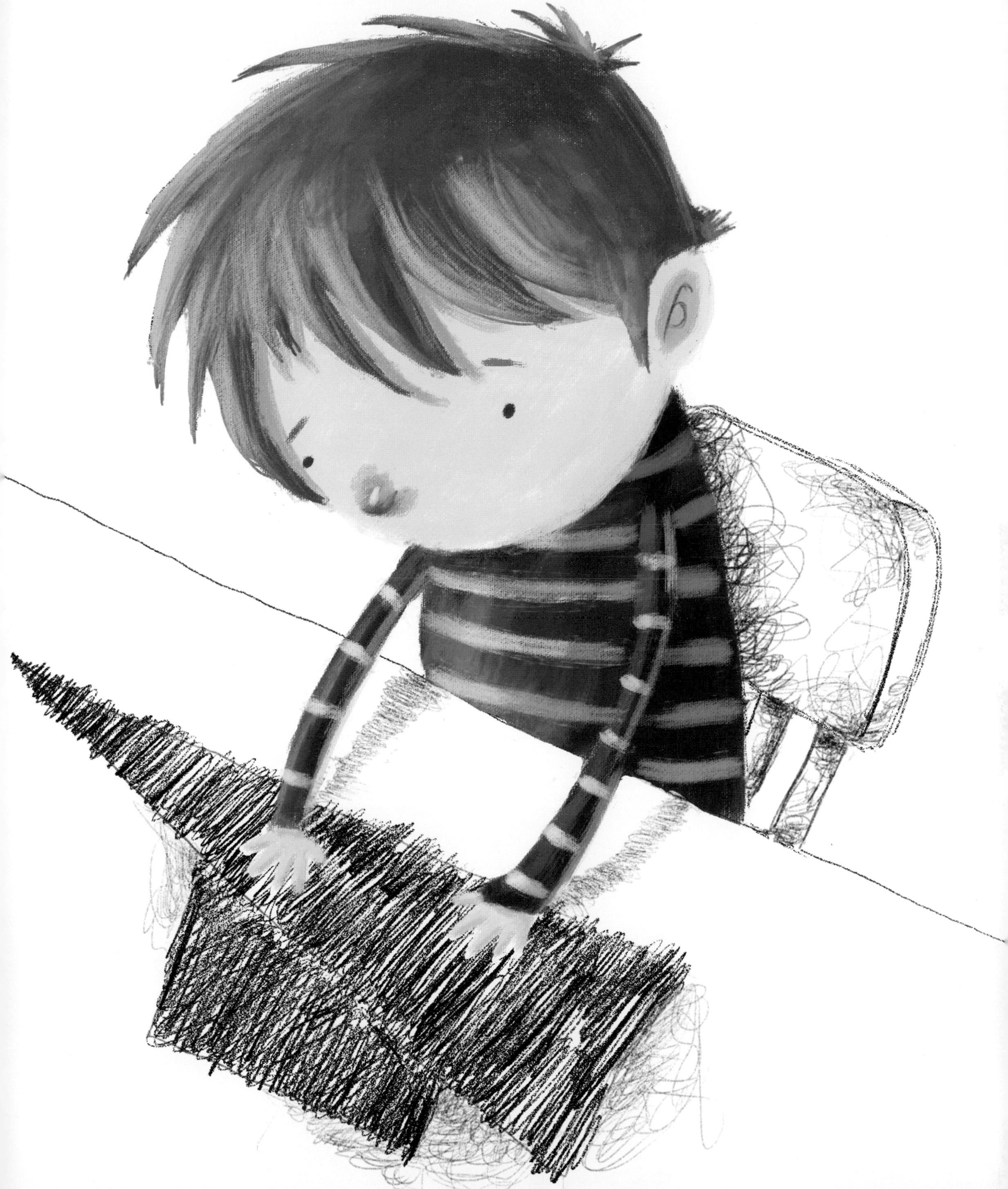

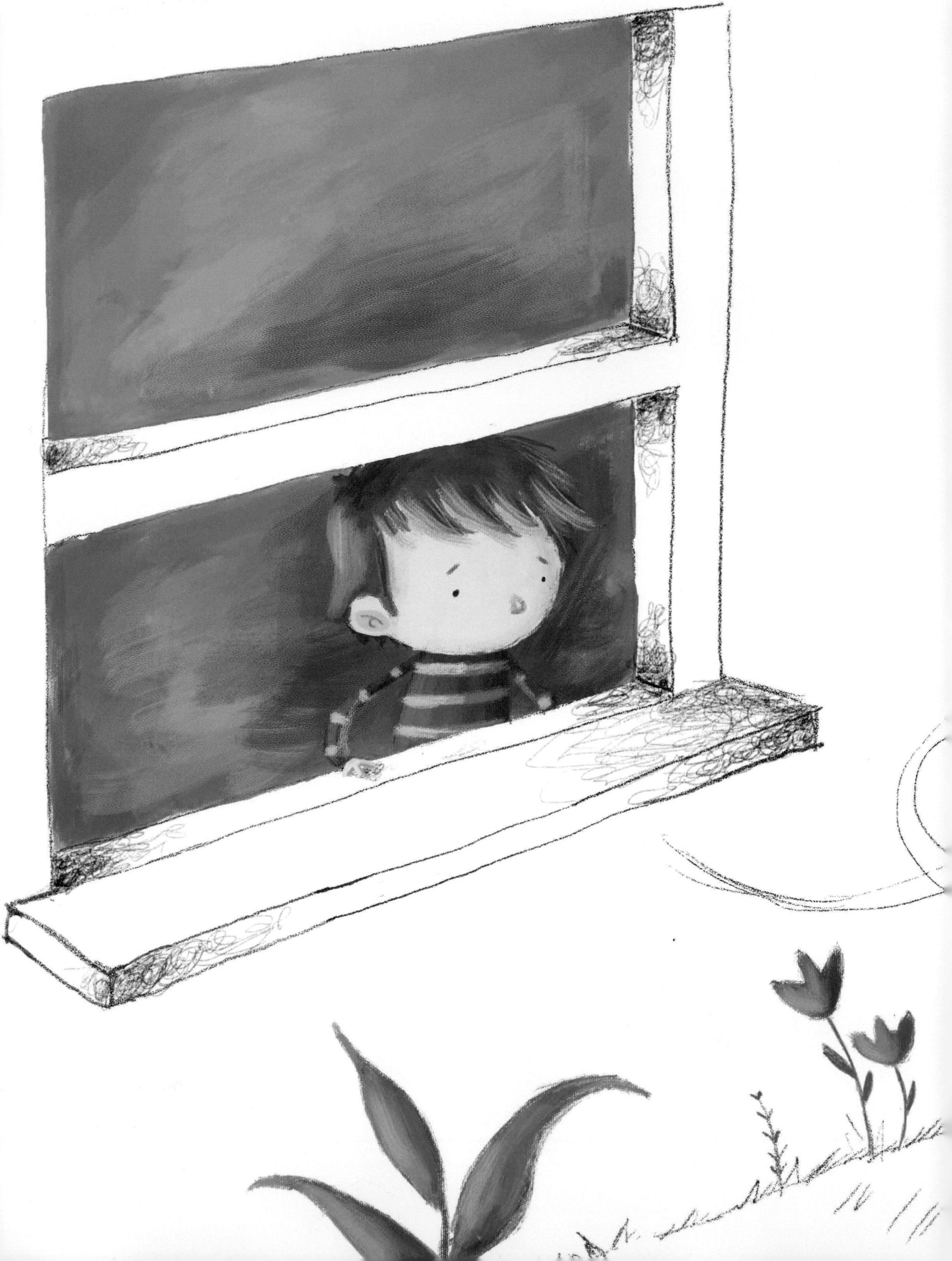

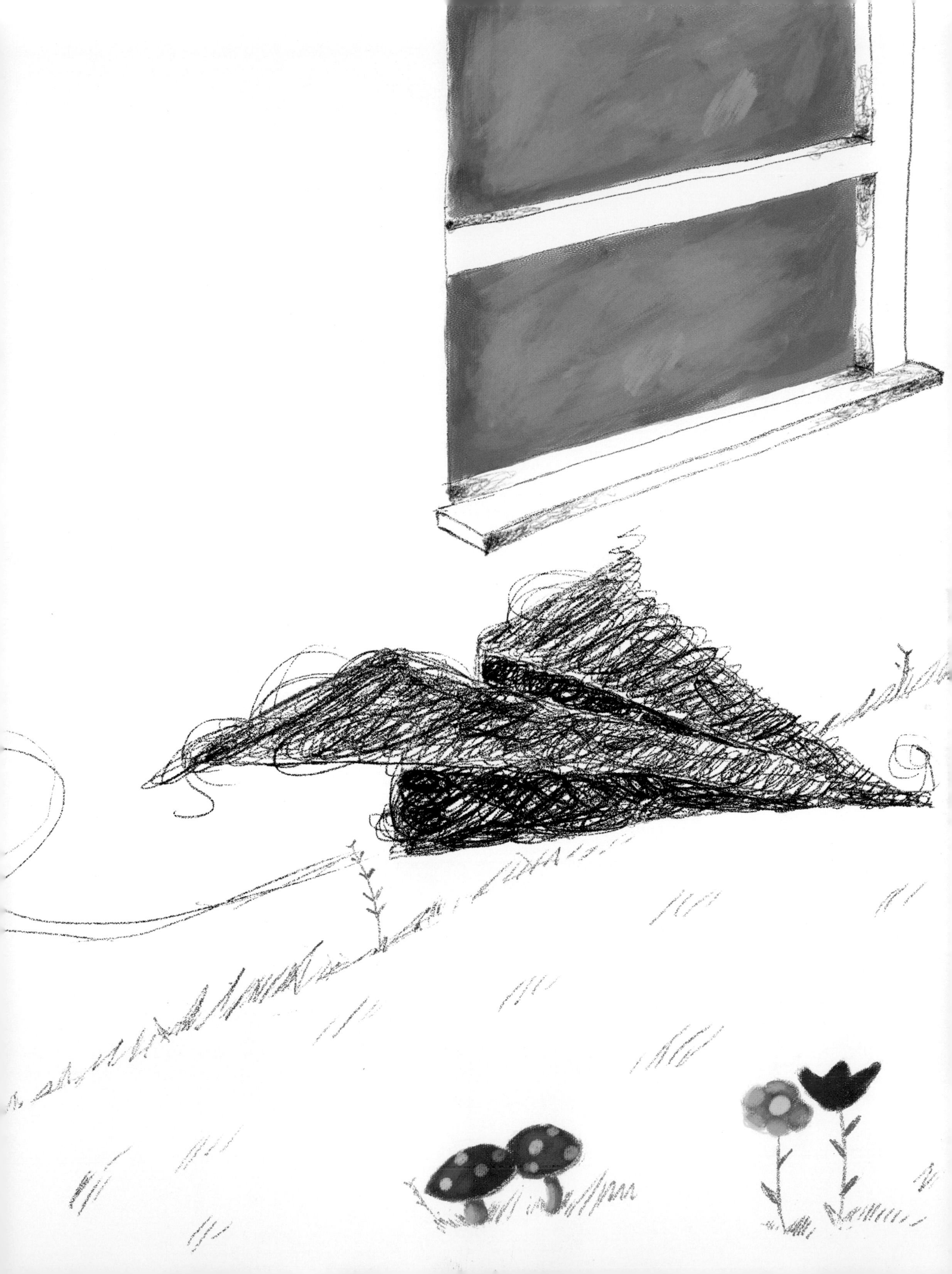

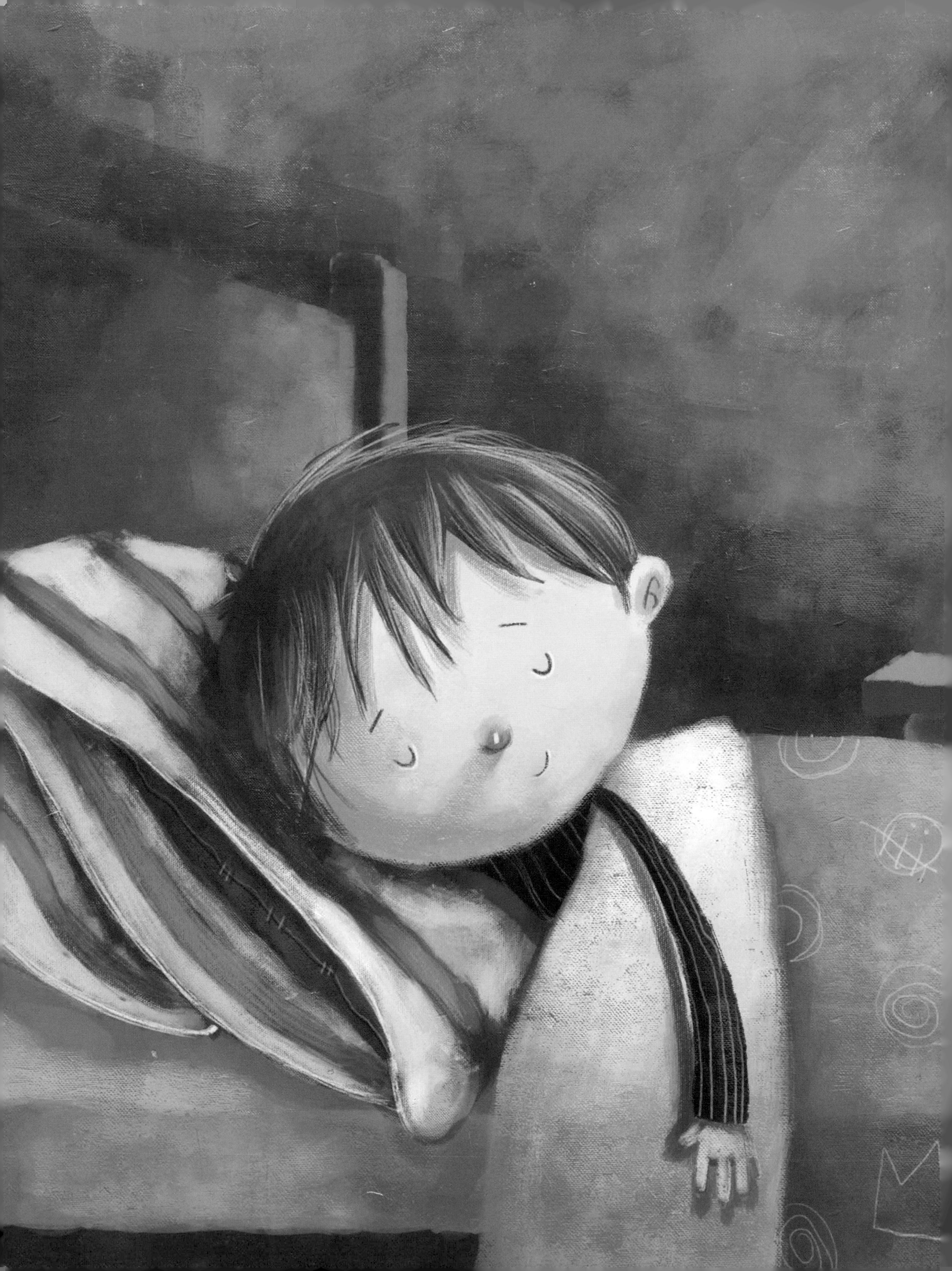

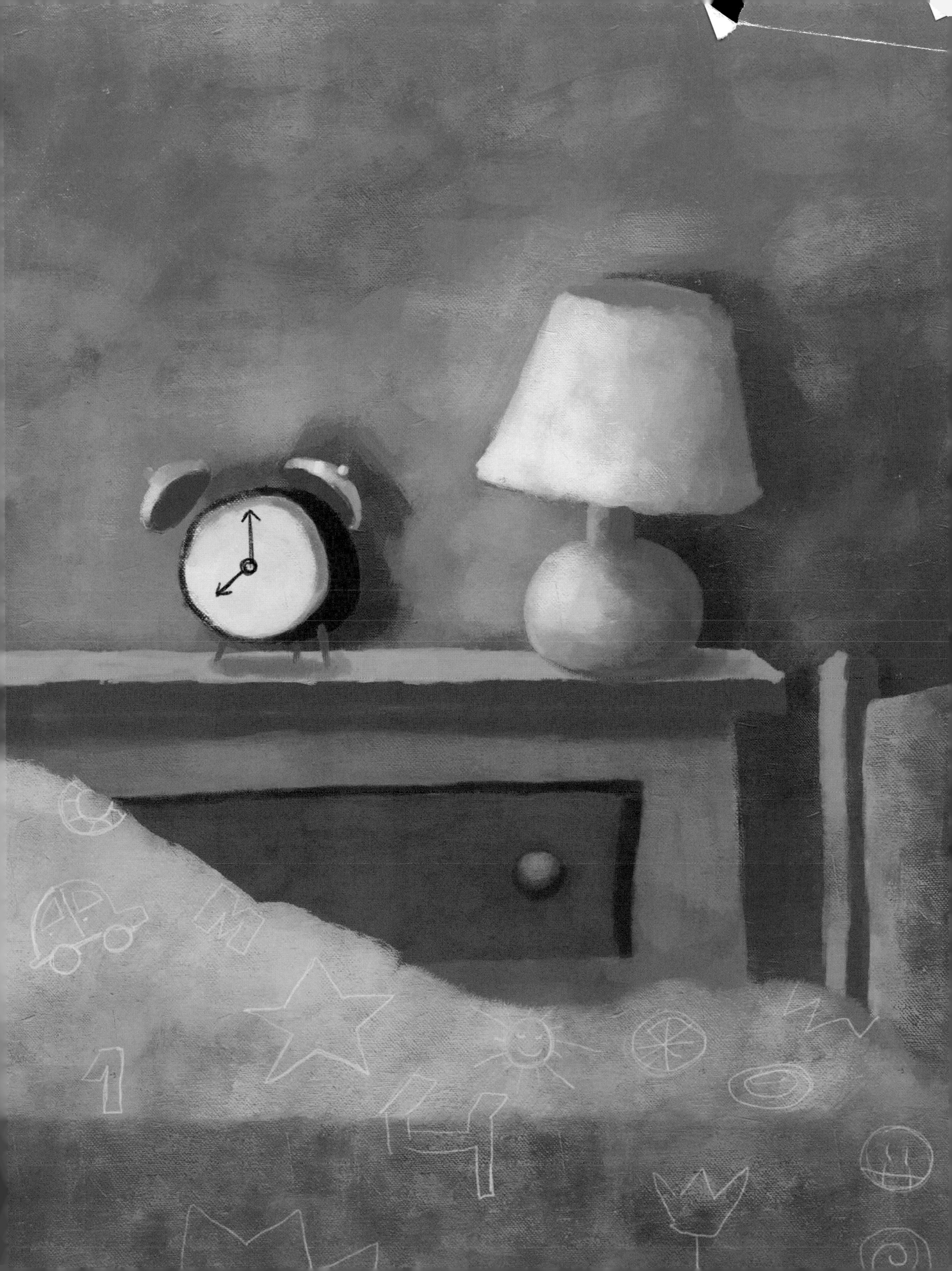

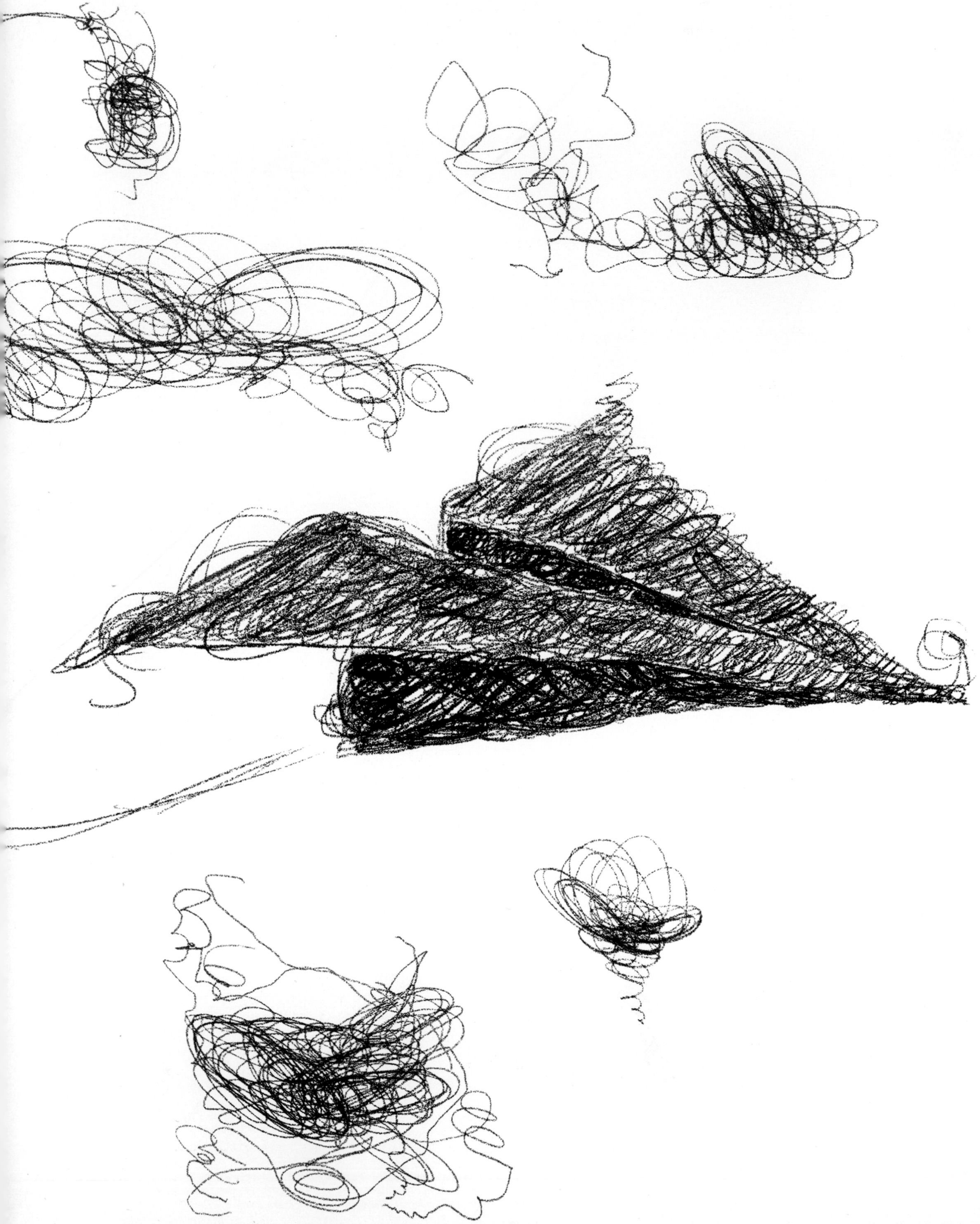